"Remember what I told you last night?" Nick said.

She glanced at him.

"You're not alone, Sarah. We'll find Emma."

"Emma is sixteen and my responsibility, and I'm the only one left alive now who knows how impulsive she can be. Maybe I'm overreacting, but I can't take any chances with her."

"I'm catching on pretty quickly to her tactics. Let me take some of this load, okay? You won't be any good to yourself or Emma if you give in to panic." He placed a hand over hers.

Sarah felt the warmth of Nick's hand melting into her icy fingers. She hadn't realized how tightly she was wound. She shook her head. "I can handle this."

"You lost both your parents and suddenly became the guardian of a very headstrong teenager who also, most likely, has PTSD mingling with grief after discovering their deaths might have been murder. I'm so sorry my efforts to get to the bottom—"

"Enough with the poor-little-Sarah routine, okay? I'll deal with it."

Because getting to the bottom of things was what Sarah was so afraid of.

HANNAH ALEXANDER

is the pseudonym of husband-and-wife writing team Cheryl and Mel Hodde (pronounced "Hoddee"). When they first met, Mel had just begun his new job as an E.R. doctor in Cheryl's hometown, and Cheryl was working on a novel. Cheryl's matchmaking pastor set them up on an unexpected blind date at a local restaurant. Surprised by the sneak attack, Cheryl blurted the first thing that occurred to her, "You're a doctor? Could you help me paralyze someone?" Mel was shocked. "Only temporarily, of course," she explained when she saw his expression. "And only fictitiously. I'm writing a novel."

They began brainstorming immediately. Eighteen months later they were married, and the novels they set in fictitious Ozark towns began to sell. The first novel in the Hideaway series won the prestigious Christy Award for Best Romance in 2004.

COLLATERAL DAMAGE

HANNAH ALEXANDER

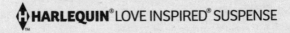
HARLEQUIN® LOVE INSPIRED® SUSPENSE

Recycling programs for this product may not exist in your area.

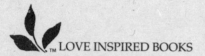

LOVE INSPIRED BOOKS

ISBN-13: 978-0-373-67613-2

COLLATERAL DAMAGE

This edition published by arrangement with Love Inspired Books.

® and TM are trademarks of Love Inspired Books, used under license. Trademarks indicated with ® are registered in the United States Patent and Trademark Office, the Canadian Trade Marks Office and in other countries.

www.Harlequin.com

Printed in U.S.A.

"For I know the plans I have for you," declares the Lord, "plans to prosper you and not to harm you, plans to give you hope and a future."
—*Jeremiah* 29:11

This book is dedicated to those who spend so much of their time and finances to keep a piece of history alive in Jolly Mill Park, Missouri. May God be with those on this special private park board, who strive to remind us that we are always making history.

ONE

The warning shriek of a siren accompanied a blur of Missouri roadside shrubs and the flash of red-blue-red in Sarah Russell's rearview mirror. She dabbed at her wet face with the cuff of her sleeve. Another blast of sound and flash of lights near her back bumper told her she was busted. "Oh, sure," she muttered. "Don't go after the real speeders. Pick on me."

All she needed right now, atop everything else, was public humiliation—it would be bad enough when the whole Russell family found out she'd lost Emma after having custody for only three weeks. And she hadn't been speeding. True, squealing tire rubber on the road was never a good idea, and she should have known better than to attempt highway traffic while fighting tears that flowed faster than her speedometer, but still…

With a wet sniffle, she pulled to the shoulder of Highway 60. A few more seconds and she'd have been out of the Sikeston city limits and on her way toward Jolly Mill.

She closed her eyes and focused on breathing deeply. The word *murder* reverberated through her mind in time with her heartbeat. Impossible. Couldn't be! But what if it was true? Innocent, trusting sixteen-year-old Emma was headed toward disaster in more ways than one.

Sarah fumbled in her purse for a tissue and was blowing her nose when a uniformed figure stepped from the cruiser behind her. She lowered the window, winced at the squeak she'd never had repaired and looked up—into the face of her cousin, John Fred Russell.

"Oh, John." She nearly burst into fresh tears at the sight of the man who'd been like a brother since her family moved here. Among all the Russell cousins, John was her favorite. A person couldn't spit on the sidewalk in this town without the whole Russell clan hearing about it, but John had kept silent for years about her most devastating secret. He was a true man.

"Sarah Fey Russell," he muttered with a voice of resignation.

"John, this isn't a good time. Please, just let me go. Didn't you recognize my car?"

"All I saw was a set of taillights weaving back and forth on the road like a flag in a high wind," he drawled, wiggling his hand in the air. "But yes, when you finally stopped, I knew it was you."

A pickup truck sped past. He glanced toward the

receding vehicle then sighed and returned his attention to her. "I have to ask, of course, so just tell me you haven't suddenly taken up drinking and driving for recreation." Again, the dry tone, his southeastern Missouri accent as pronounced as usual. His typical expression of serenity was firmly in place, which meant he knew she wouldn't need to breathe into a tube.

She shook her head, sniffed and dabbed at a few stray tears with her sleeve.

He leaned over and peered at her face more closely. "Hey, cuz." His tone softened. "You crying? What's wrong?"

He'd been a rock since Mom and Dad died three weeks ago.... Could Emma be right? Was it possible their deaths weren't just a tragic accident? "I've already blown the guardianship."

"How?"

"I've lost Emma."

"What?"

Sarah reached toward the passenger seat for the printout of the long email she'd found after arriving home from her final, long day of teachers' meetings to end the school year.

He took the sheet and squinted. "Wow. Save me some time. Give me the short version."

"She's driving across the state to Jolly Mill to investigate a rumor that the explosion that killed Mom and Dad was intentional."

John hunkered down, eyes wide. "Someone thinks your parents were murdered?"

More tears surfaced as Sarah's throat threatened to close. It was too fresh. Only three weeks since her world had shattered. "Nick Tyler suspects something. He's Aunt Peg's son."

"She was the other person killed in the first explosion. You've mentioned Nick. You two were best buds when you lived there, right?"

Sarah hesitated. If John only knew. And perhaps he should. "If Nick suspects something, then I believe there's something to suspect." She held up Emma's note. "There was another explosion the next day and another woman died—a nurse in an infirmary not far from the conference center where Mom and Dad and Aunt Peg were killed."

John let out a long, low whistle. "There's no police force in Jolly Mill."

"That's probably why Nick's staying with his dad for a while, just to keep an eye on things."

"If that's where Emma's going, will she be safe there?"

Sarah leaned her forehead against the steering wheel, trying not to think about it. "Her email to me was time-stamped two-thirteen. If she left soon after, she could be there by now."

He looked at his watch. "Seven now. Yep, she could be." He blew out a puff of air. "What on earth did that girl think there was to investigate?"

"You know Emma. She wants to be a police officer like her cousin John, so it's your fault."

"You've tried calling her, of course."

"She's not answering her cell."

Another car sped past, and John grimaced. "Wish we weren't already two people short tonight. I should go with you. Have you spoken with Nick?"

"All he and I have exchanged since our family moved away from there are sympathy notes after the explosion. Emma spoke with him on the phone."

"Well, okay, but he *is* a son grieving the death of his mother. Even the most solid people I know can go a little off-kilter when they're reeling from that kind of shock."

"Two explosions a day apart, John. That's not too much of a stretch. And, John, there's more." Sarah hesitated, closing her eyes. "Please promise this doesn't go anywhere."

He leaned forward, elbows resting on the car door until he was eye level with Sarah. "How much worse can it get?"

"I know under the circumstances this shouldn't be an issue, but I'm pretty sure he's Emma's father."

There was a long moment of silent shock that froze her cousin's face like a statue. "What do you mean you're *pretty sure?*"

"There was a going-away party for Shelby and me. Someone spiked the soda with ecstasy right there under the guard of chaperones and everything. Anyway, that night's a huge blur, but—"

John interrupted with a groan. "It's okay, I don't need the details. I'd like to wring the neck of the scum who did that to a bunch of innocent kids. Does Nick know she's his?"

Sarah closed her eyes and shook her head, allowing the impact of her past to hit her full force. All these years, at the urging of her parents, she'd been encouraged to treat Emma like her surprise baby sister, born just after Sarah and her twin, Shelby, turned seventeen. They never knew she suspected that Nick was the one. Who else could it have been? How her family had sacrificed for her wild, childish heart and for someone's nasty practical joke.

"Sarah?"

"You know how it was. Mom and Dad believed if they didn't adopt her I wouldn't go to college, wouldn't have the chance Shelby had. I have nothing to go on but memories of seeking Nick out at the party—they're fuzzy, at best. Everyone found out about the spiked soda, so my parents always knew I'd been caught up in something I had no control over."

"So you can't be sure it was him."

"He was the only one I'd have even gotten close to. He was the only one. Ever. She looks like him."

John sighed. "This one's a doozy, Sarah Fey, I've gotta tell you."

"I'm worried about Emma. She's still such a little girl in so many ways. It's partially my fault she's been so sheltered. I spent so much time with her—"

"You're good for her, Sarah. You practically gave up dating. In fact, I think she was smothered, if you ask me."

"Didn't ask." Still, his words soothed her. "So, you letting me go? My tire went off the shoulder, that's all. I'm fine." Jolly Mill, a five hour drive from Sikeston, seemed as far away as the moon right now. "If Emma reaches Nick and he sees the family resemblance in person—"

"You can't stop her now." He patted her arm. "Maybe it's time she knew—"

"Don't even say it."

"As her sister, you may not be able to control her, but if she knows you're her birth mother and that you love her like a mother loves a child—"

"That's the last thing she needs. You know how tender her heart is. The shock would break it all over again, especially with this question about murder hanging in the air."

"If not now—"

Sarah held a hand up. "I've been living this fiction since I was her age. For her sake I have to keep it up at least until she's strong enough to handle reality again."

John gave a heavy sigh. "At least let me find Nick's number and call him for you."

That was tempting. Talking to Nick after all these years and with such a connection hanging between them from their past—and one he knew nothing about—would be hard. But right now Emma's safety was Sarah's only concern. "I'll call him. We were once the best of friends. Can you find the number for Edward Tyler for me?"

John gave her a salute and quickstepped back to the cruiser as Sarah allowed her thoughts to dwell on Nick—something she'd stopped doing when she heard of his marriage seven years ago—and continued after Mom shared that his wife divorced him. Had it really been nearly seventeen years since she'd seen Nick? She'd cried most of the way across the state the day they left Jolly Mill. She'd had no reason to believe that she carried a child inside her—Nick's child. It had to be. The very reason she'd sought Nick out that night was to tell him how she really felt about him, that their friendship had blossomed into something so much more powerful....

Over the years, she'd often imagined Nick's dark, soul-filled eyes in his daughter's face. She'd also seen his and his father's cleft chin. Hadn't she? Would they see their own features in Emma when she showed up on their front porch? Mom had sent Aunt Peg pictures of all of them throughout the years, but Nick had left Jolly Mill for premed as soon as he graduated. Sarah's only chance to get through this with no one being the wiser was that Nick couldn't possibly recall that long-ago night any better than she did—or even as well as she did.

John returned with a slip of paper and handed it to her. "Don't talk on the phone while you're driving. I saw what you're capable of tonight."

She thanked him and reached down for the automatic window control.

"Wait, did you log on to Emma's email account, check her activity?"

"That was always Dad's job. I've tried to respect her privacy."

"My turn, then. I still have a key to the house."

"She keeps her password info taped under the lip of her desk, but she keeps her email up on the home computer, so it's not hard to log on."

"If you're gonna traipse off after Emma, the least I can do is search around and see if I can't fill in some gaps for you. Got your cell phone charged?"

What would she do without John? "I even brought my car charger. Proud of me?"

He grinned at last, then leaned in and kissed her cheek. "I've got your back, cuz. Watch for deer and call me when you get there." He straightened and stretched. "Guess I'll overlook your poor driving skills this time, but beware of weekenders. That can be a bear, even on the four-lane."

He'd pulled away in his cruiser before she edged back onto the road. This was not the time to resume panic mode, and she couldn't imagine how this night could get any worse.

Nicolas Tyler slid the hasp one more time along the riding mower's blade, sharpening it to perfection. He was rotating to the next cutting edge when the wall phone rang loudly enough for the neighbors to go deaf. His hand jerked, and the fleshy part of his right thumb encountered the newly sharpened blade.

It was a clean cut, and while the pain of it registered he couldn't help a buzz of pride at the quality of his work as he watched blood seep from the wound. He winced at the continued ringing of the phone. Should've chosen lawnmower maintenance as his primary profession twelve years ago and avoided all the frustration of education, more education, sleepless residency, divorce, frivolous lawsuits. He preferred the landscaping business to family practice for now, and solitude to marriage to a cheater.

He glared at the phone as the ringing persisted. Voice mail was turned off; everyone knew Dad's cell number. Why did Dad keep this phone out here, anyway? Didn't a guy deserve some time to himself? But then, Dad wasn't a recluse. Nick had been the one to morph to introversion when he received the notification of a frivolous malpractice lawsuit. Things had gone downhill from there.

He'd disconnected the doorbell after Chloe left

and discontinued the landline at his home in Rockford, Illinois, only a few weeks before the explosion.

The ringing stopped and Nick relaxed. Dad had his cell phone with him in case someone wanted to contact him, but he was on leave from the church. A pastor couldn't lead his flock when he was driven to his knees with grief; his church should understand that. Nick could think of no one he wanted to talk to. The neighbors knew he wasn't much of a socializer these days.

He reached for the first-aid kit in its cubicle above the work stand. A little peroxide, gauze and tape would take care of this.

He was pouring medicine into his wound when the phone jangled again. He jumped, splattering the liquid in a three foot radius and giving the garage floor an expensive cleansing. Peroxide bubbled on his hand, the gauze hovering over his thumb, tape tangling in his arm hair. With a yank and a grunt, he tore away the tape and lost a considerable amount of arm hair. And women waxed. Go figure.

He pulled out another strip of tape, secured the bandage and replaced the top on the peroxide bottle before strolling toward the phone. Maybe it was Dad. One never knew when he might run into trouble with that old pickup truck.

A quick check of the incoming number sent a shiver down Nick's spine as it had the last time he'd answered a call from Emma Russell—the name

Mark Russell flashed on the tiny screen. As if he was receiving a message from a dead man.

For that fraction of a second, as before, Nick's mind ricocheted through the grief, blackness and shock. Then he answered the phone, fully expecting to hear young Emma's voice again. She'd called him and emailed him after he'd sent the girls flowers and a sympathy card, and she'd called again today. The kid had an uncanny sense of compassion for one so young. It surprised him that he didn't mind talking to her.

"Hello, Nick?"

He hesitated. Not Emma. Too mature for a sixteen-year-old. He found his voice, but only barely. "Is this...Sarah?"

For a moment, there was no reply. Sarah was the quiet one, the twin who'd always remained in the shadows at her own insistence. Though he hadn't heard her voice for many years, he recalled the beautiful script on her sympathy card after the tragedy.

"I'm sorry to bother you." Her voice continued to wobble.

Not how he remembered her at all. "Bother? You? Never." Her loss had obviously taken a heavy toll. "Kind of startled. I thought it was Emma. I saw your father's...uh...name on the caller ID." Oh brother, just what she needed.

"Yeah, Dad had all of us on a family plan for our cells. He wanted his name to show up when we called anybody, especially when Emma called boys. Leave it to Dad to be overprotective."

"I remember Mark could be intimidating when boys came around."

"Not with you, of course. Listen, um, I need to warn you that you might have company soon, if you don't already."

"Company?"

"Emma."

"She's coming here?"

"I'm on my way there, too. She told me about your theory.... The explosions? Murder?"

He wanted to bang his head against the wall in self-reproach. "I'm sorry, Sarah. I didn't mean for this to reach you or Emma. You're struggling enough. I was looking for help from neighbors and friends here in Jolly." That was how a newly minted recluse did things—online.

"You believe it."

"I...have my suspicions."

"Too coincidental to have two explosions like that." As she spoke, her voice regained the steadiness he remembered from their teen years. "Two days in a row."

"Exactly." Why hadn't he crawled from his hidey-hole here at Dad's and gone door-to-door and faced all those neighbors instead of setting up that blog? "I was hoping to talk to you about all this after I'd found out more. You're sure about Emma? She called me today, a little after noon, and she didn't say anything about coming here."

"You'll understand better once you meet her. She thinks she's going to help. She left me an extended email explaining it, which I didn't receive until I got home from work tonight. I'm sure that was her intention."

"I'm sorry. I knew that controversial blog could stir up trouble, but not for you."

"So you were trying to gather information from the community?"

"Exactly." And it was the very community that was never the same after Sarah was gone. The weight of seventeen years dropped from his shoulders for a few seconds, and he recalled with exquisite clarity the impact of Sarah's presence in his life—and the dark pit that remained in his heart after Mark Russell moved his family away to St. Louis. By the time Nick was in college, he heard they'd moved to Sikeston so Mark could take a job as pastor of a congregation again.

After a brief hesitation, Sarah said, "I don't understand. Didn't the investigator blame the explosions on gas leaks from faulty pipes?"

"Two gas leaks in two days? Not likely. The investigator was a new kid, not only wet behind the ears, but as slick as if he'd just hatched. His father's a local judge, and the kid—his name's Chaz Collins—missed some inspection reports that showed no cracks where he indicated. He's off the case, and right now there's no one to fill his shoes. The sheriff's busy chasing meth labs, and you know Jolly Mill's always been low priority."

"Chaz inspected both explosions?"

"Yep. He wouldn't look me in the eye when I spoke with him."

"Could he have had something to do with it? You know, start a fire, cause an explosion so he could make the judgment and prove his worth?"

"And kill people in the process? Chaz and his family attend Dad's church."

"Just because he's a churchgoer doesn't mean he's a good boy."

Nick hesitated. Emma was on her way here and Sarah was following her; they'd find out the worst as soon as they arrived. "The problem is, Sarah, Chaz is nowhere to be found."

There was a soft intake of breath.

"There's a search under way. His parents called yesterday, and they're frantic."

"You think he did find something incriminating?" Sarah asked.

"Judging by his behavior, I'm almost sure of it."

For a moment Sarah didn't speak, and Nick recalled her tendency to choose her words carefully. In that way she was very different from her twin, who would chatter to anyone and everyone in school—Shelby, the popular twin.

"You think someone might have threatened him," Sarah said.

"Seems possible."

"A gas leak could have developed after the last inspection," she said.

Nick shook his head, though of course she couldn't see him. "Leo Larner constructed that conference building above code thirty years ago. Dad even did his own inspection before each event. He's cautious that way. There were no faulty pipes."

There was a soft sigh. "But why our parents?"

"I don't know yet. You know they always stay to clean up after the others leave, but Dad just happened to get a call on his cell while they were working, and walked outside—that building never had good reception. That's when the place exploded. It's eating at him."

"Who called?"

"He said it sounded like someone crying, but when Gerard Vance—he's an ex-cop—had a check run on the number, it was from a burn phone. No name connected to it."

There was another long silence. "So it was an attack on either Mom or Dad or Aunt Peg by someone who definitely wanted to spare Edward. But why him specifically? Does he have any ideas?"

"No, and it's torturing him."

"Why the nurse in the infirmary the next day?"

"All I can figure is that she might've been close enough to look out her window and see something before the explosion at the conference center."

"So she could've been killed because she was an eye witness?"

"It's all wild conjecture at this point. She wasn't even from here—she was from Texas—so unless someone followed her here...I just don't know. It's why I got involved, and Gerard Vance is helping me. He was the nurse's employer."

More silence.

He gave Sarah time to assimilate what he'd told her, then frowned as the silence continued. "Hello? Are we disconnected?"

"I'm...here. I'm trying to grasp it all, and I can't yet." Sarah sighed. Sniffed. It was a wet sniff that told him how hard this was hitting her, and then it hit him, too. Again. As it did several times a day. Mom was gone. "I know Edward's got to be torn up about this."

"He just got out of the house for the first time last Sunday. Your cousin and her friends are all worried about him, bringing food." Carmen Delaney, Mrs. Russell's cousin, had been good about keeping friends and neighbors abreast of how the Russells were doing since they left Jolly Mill.

Carmen was also the one who'd broken the news about Emma's birth nine months after their family left

Jolly Mill. There were still moments when Nick wondered about the timing of her birth, and tried to weave his mind through the cloudy memories of Sarah's twin, Shelby, on the night of the party. Nothing had ever come of his attempts. "I hear from Carmen that Emma's an impulsive, intelligent, inquisitive kid."

Sarah gave a soft groan. "Emma. She's…amazing. She's also a handful. I'm afraid you'll find out what I mean soon."

"Headstrong, obviously. I can't believe she would let you worry like this."

"We had a little spat last night, and that doesn't often happen. In her note she told me she needed more information about how Mom and Dad died. I haven't been able to reach her on her cell."

He leaned back in the chair, focusing, for a moment, on the gentle wave of Sarah's voice—recalling her quiet but welcome presence from their teen years. That voice had a musical quality that always soothed the soul, though he couldn't miss the distress in it now. "The girl has her mother's stubborn streak."

There was a soft gasp, and then, "What?"

"Sorry, Sarah. I didn't mean to diss your mother. I just remembered my mom always talked about Lydia Russell and her determination to get things done. Mom admired her."

"Oh. Thank you. Yes, Dad always said Shelby and I inherited Mom's strong will."

"As did Emma, obviously."

"I need to get her back home to Sikeston," Sarah said.

"Meaning I've frightened you."

"You'd better believe it. I can't believe the sheriff's department isn't even investigating."

"He has very little manpower with all the budget cuts, and there's a lot for him to cover in our county. Don't worry, Gerard's got a good eye on things, and if Emma shows up I'll take care of her."

What was it about Sarah's vulnerable presence over the phone that brought out his old protective instincts? What was it about connecting with her that made him see the man—or lesser man—he'd become? He wanted to be that former man, who could be counted on for help, who actually wanted to help instead of search for ulterior motives behind every word. Divorce and the lawsuit had changed him, and he disliked the curmudgeon he'd become.

"Sarah? I'm serious about this. You're not alone."

There was another sniff. "Thanks, Nick. I'm glad I called."

He closed his eyes at the memories Sarah's voice resurrected. It sounded as if he might have company at any time, and he couldn't help remembering her eyes—the color of the ocean on a cloudy day—and the tenderness of her heart, which she'd taken such pains to conceal behind her dyed-black hair, Goth makeup and clothing as a teenager.

Why had he allowed Shelby's effusive, chatter-box ways to distract his attention from Sarah for even a few moments? And what kind of kid had he been to momentarily fall for externals at exactly the wrong time?

For the first time in many months, Nick found himself thinking about someone besides himself and his personal battles. "It's going to be okay." He only had to convince himself of that, and it was threatening to become an impossible task.

TWO

The shadows of the night whipped past Sarah's headlights as the depth and warmth of Nick's reassuring voice continued to echo in her head. The rhythm of his words soothed her into a near-trance. Her eyes were half shut when a deer flitted across the road in the far reach of the high beams, shocking her awake. She hit the brakes, glad the lateness of the night had emptied this highway of most automobiles. This part of Missouri was notorious for its nightlife; nocturnal animals could outnumber cars on the road.

Another deer leaped past the beams, and another, and she braced herself, pressing harder on the pedal.

The chirp of her cell phone claimed her attention as the small herd disappeared into the blackness of forest south of the road. When she answered, she heard John's wide-awake voice.

"Got something, Sarah. Are you hands-free?"

"No, but there's no traffic."

"Pull over so we can talk. I'll wait."

"John, stop being such a policeman. I'm practically stopped already." No need to mention the deer. She pulled far off the shoulder into the grass beyond. "Just tell me what you've got."

"Listen, how much time does Emma spend online? I've warned her about the danger of predators."

Already startled awake by the deer, Sarah felt her muscles tense. "What did you find?"

"I've got a couple more names and addresses for you. Did you know a man by the name of Alec Thompson? His comment on Nick's blog was, 'Emma, I know your family.' It was as if he was trying to lure her into a conversation. I'm getting ready to call Sheriff Moritz over there to give him a heads-up on—"

"No, don't. Alec's okay." The lack of sleep, the worry about Emma, the reconnections to the past were all catching up with her.

"You know the guy?"

"His family owned several businesses in Jolly Mill when we lived there, and he dated a friend of mine. You know, I haven't been there in over sixteen years, but I still think of Jolly Mill as my hometown. We're talking about a small community, where everyone knows practically everyone else. The thought that someone I might have known could've been a killer—"

"And that Emma's headed there?"

Sarah gritted her teeth. Yes. Exactly. "And she won't answer her phone."

"Sorry she's doing this to you. I know you think your old hometown's the best place on the planet, but things change over the years."

"Not so much. Those explosions would have stirred up the whole community, even though we've been gone since Emma's conception. People are going to talk, and when they talk, some questions might be answered. Nick's blog was a good idea." Sarah opened the window and allowed the cool night air to rush into the car. "Emma wasn't there when I called Nick."

"I'm sorry, cuz. You know we'll all be praying for you to have a safe trip."

"I'm not even sure I can make it there tonight."

"Why not?"

Sarah took a deep breath of fresh air and watched the fog of moisture drift through the moonlight when she exhaled. "I barely slept after a little tiff with Emma last night. It's catching up with me now."

"Where are you?"

"Close to Cabool."

"Only halfway. You'd better get thee to a safe hotel and get some rest. You won't do Emma any good if you have a wreck."

Sarah needed coffee. The clock in her dashboard told her it was nine-thirty. Two and a half more hours of driving, and she still had no idea if she would find Emma when she arrived at her destination.

"I checked out Nick a little more thoroughly," John said.

"How?"

"It's all about computers these days, cuz. It's there—you just have to find it."

"So…what did you find?"

John chuckled. "Can't help yourself, can you? I have a feeling you might be carrying some glowing embers for the guy."

She felt herself smiling in spite of everything. "John."

"Sorry, but if Nick wants you to know about *his* business, he'll have to tell you himself."

"Did you read his blog?"

"Yep. Cuz, don't freak, but I'm afraid he might be onto something. He asked for information about a toxin leak many years ago in a river about twenty miles from Jolly Mill, but unless he comes up with more there, I think that's a no-go. Still, something's up."

"Nick didn't say anything about that." She shoved open the door, stepped out into the cool night air and was nearly sideswiped by a speeding motorcycle. She ran around the front of her car and into the ditch on the other side, her footing precarious.

"Breathe, Sarah."

"I'm breathing." But this was feeling too real.

"What's wrong?" John asked.

"Someone intentionally called Edward just before the explosion. Everyone in town probably knows about the bad cell reception in that conference center, so they must have known he would step outside. Our parents were best friends. Those meetings they had every year? They used to hold them in a place on Spring River until that toxin scare. After that, Dad made the decision to change the venue to the conference center at Jolly." She stepped from the soggy, weed-filled ditch into the heavier darkness of the woods. "The man who owned the place on the river killed himself after the dioxin spill at Verona, and Dad blamed himself."

"What? Why?"

"Because when Dad withdrew from the Spring River center, others did, too."

"That's no reason for Uncle Mark to blame himself. He was protecting people."

"What if someone else blamed him for that poor man's suicide? The guy lost his income and lost hope."

There was a hesitation. "Okay, listen, Sarah, I've got some vacation days coming to me. I could call the chief, see if—"

"No, you don't need to go to Jolly. You need to get that detective position."

"This is getting a little too much for nonprofessionals to handle."

"Nick told me there's an ex-cop he's working with."

There was a heavy sigh. "Guess you know where to find Nick."

"I practically lived at their house half the time when I was a kid."

"I'll update you if I find anything else. You stop and rest. And, Sarah—"

"I know. You've got my back."

"That's right, cuz, I've got your back."

The gentle melody of Sarah's voice echoed in Nick's mind instead of the scrape of the hasp he eased over one of the push mower blades. She was coming here. The last time he'd seen her in person she'd had long, Goth black hair and her beautiful eyes had been overwhelmed by the heavy makeup. How would she look as a grown woman?

He realized he wanted to see her, looked forward to it.

Once again breathing in the scent of motor oil, dried grass and gasoline in the two-car garage, he glanced at the clock and wondered where Dad was. For the time being, both of them had been parking their vehicles in the driveway so there would be room for Nick to work on the mowers and lawn-care equipment he'd purchased two weeks ago. Dad had pulled Mom's car around back to a shed where he wouldn't have to look at it every time he stepped to the kitchen window. He refused to drive it. Instead, he continued to rattle around in the twenty-year-old Ford pickup he'd always driven. Small-town pastors didn't bring in millions from their congregations.

Nick's thoughts returned to Sarah and the stress evident in her voice, her sorrow over the loss of her parents, the love he'd heard between the lines for her younger sister. Nothing felt quite real tonight. Except for Sarah.

Like Dad, Nick was still grieving hard over Mom's death. After the shocks in life these past couple of years, he was still scrambling to catch up with a lot of things. Maybe he was grasping for something from the past—something of comfort. If nothing else, Sarah's presence, even over the airway, had served to take him back to a gentler time when she was his friend and confidante, solid and serene and capable of gentle humor. Her twin had the infectious giggle and quips that kept everyone else laughing, but sometimes it was at the expense of others. Sarah never did that.

He was turning the rotary to the next blade when he heard the unique murmur of a Volkswagen Beetle engine pull to a stop outside the house. The engine died. He frowned. He'd neglected to ask Sarah what kind of car Emma drove.

A car door closed, and he was waiting for the chime of the doorbell when a knock against the garage door three feet away startled him.

"Dr. Tyler?"

Young. Feminine. Sounded a little shaky. And he couldn't ignore the title. Respectful, as she'd seemed online and on the phone. Emma. He hesitated, relieved beyond expectation that she'd arrived safely, but for Sarah's sake unwilling to make her entrance an easy one. She must have seen his work lights seeping out from beneath the big door. It was why she hadn't gone to the front.

"Hello?" she called.

"Yes?" He drawled the word slowly.

"Um, I'm Emma? You know, Russell?"

He waited for more explanation.

"We emailed and talked to each other a few times about our mothers?" she continued. "They were friends. And you went to school with my sisters. The twins? Do you remember Shelby and Sarah Russell?"

Shaking his head, amazed she'd think he wouldn't remember, he grabbed a slightly stained work rag and wiped as much grass and oil as he could from his hands. "Don't you live in Sikeston?"

"Well, yeah, but I came here to see you."

Sarah was right: this one was a handful. "And Sarah's waiting for you in the car?"

"Um, no. I'm by myself."

"What! How old are you, young lady?" He allowed disapproval to reflect in his voice and made her wait and wonder, the way Sarah was waiting and wondering.

"I've got my license."

"You don't say."

"I've been five hours on the road—well, okay, six, no, wait, seven, because I got lost a couple of times trying to find Jolly Mill—and I didn't stop. I thought I'd run out of gas before I could find your place." She giggled nervously. "You people sure like to keep to yourselves, don't you? You got a bathroom? I really have to—"

"Does Sarah even know where you are?" He was tempted to keep stalling. Sweet and genuine as she seemed, the kid could use some discipline.

"Um, yes?"

"You don't sound so sure of that." He reached for the button to raise the door but didn't push it. "You're trying to tell me she sent you driving across the state all by yourself? I would never have believed the Sarah Russell I knew would be so irresponsible." He silently apologized to Sarah.

"Um, well, no, she didn't. But she knows where I am now, anyway. I'm sure she does, because I sent her an email." There was a soft moan.

Nick grinned, relenting at last, though Dad was still gone and it was totally against the unwritten rules of preacher-kid conduct for a teenager to visit a single, grown, male nonfamily member alone in a house.

He pushed the button that started the garage door's slow and noisy ascent. Light from the garage revealed bare legs to the knees—though the temperature certainly didn't warrant shorts this late at this time of year—and bare arms. He could practically see goose bumps from twenty feet away.

Then her shoulders and head came into view. Long, dark brown hair; deep, familiar brown eyes; the slight curves of a girl younger than sixteen. Those curves were covered demurely enough. She had the wide, uncertain gaze of a teenager who knew she was probably in trouble and was having second and third thoughts about acting out. She was the image of her older sister, Shelby—would be the image of Sarah at that age, as well, of course, if Sarah had kept her natural hair color and wiped the glop from her face.

He sucked in his breath as memories accosted him—fuzzy memories of a party and of Shelby Russell and once again a haunting at the back of his mind over Emma's birth nine months later, despite being assured she belonged to Mr. and Mrs. Russell. He'd seen pictures of her and wondered, but Shelby had made it clear she wanted nothing to do with him. Had that night even happened? Maybe Sarah could clear things up.

"You wanted to talk to me, remember?" Emma rushed into the garage, hugging herself and doing the girly dance of urgency. "You said so in your last post." She sounded like Shelby, too, and her voice held that breathless, excited quality that Shelby had used when she was cheerleader their sophomore and junior years.

"I said I wanted to talk to you and Sarah. Big difference. You should have waited until she could come with you. Why didn't you tell me you were coming when you called?"

She continued to dance and hug herself, the dainty lines of her face making it clear she was struggling with guilt and agony. "I'm sorry. If I'd told you, you wouldn't have let me come. And I know Sarah wouldn't have come. She always has some excuse to stay home. A-always better to do the deed and then apologize later than to ask for permission first and then disobey, r-right?" She was trying to sound so blasé, and failing so prettily.

He suppressed a grin. "Really? I always heard that was the coward's way out. You couldn't have learned that from the Sarah Russell I knew."

"From a cousin in Sikeston. You got a jacket or something? You didn't tell me you lived on the North Pole." She was still trying to brave it out, though he could read her emotions from the quick blinking and sniffing, the wobbling of her dimpled chin.

"I live on the same latitude as you, so you should have known better." He grabbed his sweatshirt and tossed it to her, then glanced out the door. Every resident along Capps Creek would know about this visit before breakfast in the morning, not that any of their neighbors would think ill of him—not that he even cared for his own sake. He did care about Dad, however. As good and kind as most folks were in this town, at least one sin dwelt in abundance in this place: gossip.

"B-bathroom?"

He nodded toward the door to the house. "Down the hall and to the left."

She crashed through the door before he finished talking. "Thank you!"

He stood where he was for a moment, amazed, charmed, far too curious and somehow, beyond all else, comforted, and he didn't even know why. Time to share some of that comfort with someone who needed it more than he did. He picked up the receiver and dialed Sarah's number.

Sarah's eyelids pulled downward as if ten-pound barbells weighted them. She forced them open for at least the fiftieth time and was jerking the car back onto the road when her cell rang. It awakened her only slightly. She looked in the rearview mirror and saw a wall of semitrucks coming from behind. Her foot had slid off the accelerator and she had slowed to fifty miles per hour.

Must take this call. She slapped her right cheek hard enough to water her eyes, sped up, grabbed the cell and answered. She checked the screen for a fraction of a second and allowed herself a rush of elation when she saw it was Nick. "Please tell me she's there."

"She's here."

She gasped instinctively, and her emotions rolled on a current of remembered thrill at the deep tone of comfort in his voice.

"You sound awfully tired."

Without warning, the moisture in her eyes turned into a cascade, and Sarah felt her face contort. As in Sikeston, she could barely see the road, and this four-lane was a lot busier. "I had some coffee, but that's not cutting it." She steered the car onto an exit ramp as trucks rumbled past. "Thank You, God," she whispered, unable to contain the sobs.

"Hey, Sarah, honey, it's going to be okay." He used the endearment as if without thought, but it was exactly what she needed at the moment.

It gave her time to compose herself and manage traffic. She stopped at a signal, realized it was green, turned left and followed the road toward the outer edge of Springfield. "I've been so scared. If anything happened to her I'd just..." She would want to die. "I wouldn't be able to handle it. Sorry." She took some quick gulps of air to regain control. "I don't know what I'd have done if you hadn't called, Nick. Thank you. I can never repay you, and I'm so sorry to be causing all this trouble, and—"

"You aren't the one causing trouble, Sarah. You're the one trying to manage everything on your own.

Why don't we start worrying about *you* now? Where are you?"

The flow of his words wrapped around her like a blanket held in front of a fireplace. "I just pulled off the interstate in Springfield. I don't know why I didn't just stay on Highway 60, but—"

"Springfield's a good place to stop." His voice was so gentle she felt more easing of the ache that had been with her for hours. "Is there a hotel nearby?"

"No need for that." She glanced around her at the signs, then caught a familiar logo. Airport. There would be parking. "If I could just get a little rest, freshen up, get some coffee—"

"Let me call a nearby hotel and make reservations for you. My treat. I don't want you taking any chances."

She turned right at the airport sign, then pulled to the side of the road, unable to continue. "Why are you being so kind? You don't even know me now."

"Damsels in distress, that kind of thing. Besides, how can you say I don't know a lifelong childhood buddy? How many English tests did you prep me for? Remember how well we knew the woods around town and every inch of the creek bank? Sneaking into the backside of the cave? Do you still have that little egg-sized formation I found and gave you?"

That brought a slight smile. "Sure do."

"There are brothers and sisters who don't know

each other as well as we do. Don't sixteen years count for anything?"

She smiled a little more as she recalled the happy times they'd gone fishing together, hiked the hills together and yes, even explored the cave before the adults discovered what they were doing and put a stop to it. He'd even confided in her one day when they were sixteen about a crush he'd developed on Shelby. Which had, of course, broken her heart.

"Your little sister looked kind of frightened," he said.

"Why? Did something happen?" Sarah went on immediate alert.

"She got lost, and I don't think she was sure of the reception she'd receive here."

Good. "So what kind did she get?"

"Firm but fair." There was a smile in his voice, and it warmed her.

"Don't worry, Dad will be here before long. In fact, I'll call him now and see what's keeping him, but he's out with old friends and probably forgot to check his watch."

"I'll get there as soon as I can." She dabbed at her face and resisted checking her reflection in the mirror—and why on earth would she do that? It wasn't as if he could see her. And it wasn't as if she wanted to impress him with her appearance.

"Sarah, it's late. By the time you'd get here we would all be asleep, including you, and that would be

dangerous. There are two spare rooms for guests—
you know how Mom loved company. They opened
up the attic to make another guest suite just last
year, and that's where I'll put Emma. She'll be safe
and warm and fast asleep before you could get here.
I'm serious about making reservations for you in
Springfield."

"No. Thanks, but I'll be fine." Her parents had
taken care of her responsibility all these years. This
time she could handle it herself. "You're right. I'll
get some rest and pick up Emma in the morning."

There was a short silence. "Pick her up?"

"I need to get her back home to Sikeston where
she belongs, and out of harm's way." And keep our
lives from exploding in our faces.

"You know what? I've been thinking about that.
School's out for the year, right?"

Sarah grimaced. "Yes, but Emma's been talking
about getting a summer job, and I still have so much
legal work to take care of for Mom and Dad."

"Can it wait? Dad's been through a lot these past
weeks. He's barely functioning. Same with me. You
and Emma must be reeling."

"And thus this crazy flight across Missouri."

"You don't need to be alone right now. Some time
here could help."

She grabbed a paper towel from the passenger seat
and tore off a sheet to wipe her face. Again. "Jolly
Mill isn't exactly safe."

"I had alarms put up in the house. We have a motivated neighborhood watch. Everyone's on the alert, and Gerard has a lookout from his place on the hillside above the town, complete with telescope. He's taking it seriously. Dad and I could really use your company. If it makes you feel any better, nothing else has happened since the explosions three weeks ago."

She wasn't up to an argument right now. She'd just have to convince him in the morning that she and Emma couldn't stay there. He was being a gentleman about twisting her arm, but he was twisting. Why? Part of her felt a little thrill at the thought that Nick Tyler—the guy she'd adored for years as a teenager and had thought about constantly when Emma was growing up—now wanted to reach out to her. Another part of her wanted to hide.

She couldn't respond. The longer Emma stayed in Jolly Mill, the more secrets might emerge.

"Your cousin lives right down the street from us," he said. "Carmen even packs a pistol and learned how to shoot since our ex-cop moved to town, and I know for a fact she has plenty of room in her big old house for company."

"And does Carmen have an alarm system in her house, as well?"

"Sure does. A woman living alone can't be too careful. She had it installed a week ago."

Sarah leaned her head against the headrest. On

this long drive across Missouri, why hadn't she considered what she would do about a situation like this? She hadn't expected Nick to be so generous with his time. She hadn't thought, period.

There was a sigh. "Sarah, I know you've got to be exhausted. Stop and sleep. Find a safe place. Everything's covered here, so I'll see you in the morning. Will that work for you? We'll talk about the rest then."

"It'll have to. I'm afraid my brain's on lockdown."

His voice lowered and lingered, comforting and kind. "Then sleep."

"Nick...you've always been the sweetest guy." Always.

"And you're everything I remembered you to be."

"Um...I'm not sure what that means," she said with a smile. "Good night, Nick."

"Sleep well, Sarah."

Her whole body tingled as she disconnected and placed her phone on the passenger seat. She buzzed. Excitement? Memories? Fear?

She pulled onto the deserted road that led to the airport. She would find long-term parking and catch a few hours of sleep, then wash up as well as she could, maybe even catch a shower at a nearby truck stop.

Tomorrow she could place the mantle of worry back over her shoulders.

THREE

On Saturday morning Sarah craved a shower. After a few hours of sleep at the far edge of the Springfield/Branson airport parking lot, she'd tried uncountable times to call Emma, but of course she was diverted to voice mail. The line for a shower at the truck stop in Mount Vernon was too long for her to wait.

At least she'd had a chance to brush her teeth and wash her face and grab a fast-food breakfast, so her stomach was full, but it rumbled with nerves. Last night, despite her fatigue, she'd struggled to fall asleep because she couldn't stop thinking about Nick. After all these years, she wouldn't have believed his voice would have the power to affect her. But it was more than just his voice—it was the sense of caring he'd related over the phone, the words of kindness. He'd brought back so many memories, and she caught herself wondering how their lives would have gone if they'd made different choices.

How often she'd longed to crawl back into the past and never leave town.

She pulled into Jolly Mill thirty-five minutes after finishing her breakfast and felt blasted by memories she'd believed had settled into the dust along the surrounding country roads. She admired the modest, three-bedroom brick house when she pulled into the Tyler drive. Someone had done a fine job of landscaping, with trimmed hedges, a freshly mown lawn and real grass—not the mowed weeds she'd always managed to grow on her own lawn.

She parked behind an old brown Ford pickup. Edward's truck. It had been nearly new when her family moved away. Okay, this set of recollections was hitting a little too hard.

She glimpsed a flash of bright red peeking out from behind a juniper tree at the corner of the house, and felt a quick squeeze of her chest. It was Mom's beloved VW Beetle, which Mom had been generous enough to share after Emma got her driver's license. Soon it would belong to Emma, though the title wouldn't be in her name until Sarah was convinced Emma could handle the responsibility. Maybe by the time she was twenty-one…

Lowering her squeaky driver-side window, Sarah sniffed the air. Bacon and other smoked meat scents combined with a sweetness of maple, reaching her from the restaurant a couple of blocks away, across the street from the big old wooden grain mill from which Jolly Mill had gotten its name. No telling who owned the restaurant now. Nick's uncle, Will Parker, had once made the place the most popular hangout around for local high-schoolers—therefore, Shelby had loved the place, and Sarah had seldom gone there. Nick and his cousin, Billy, Will's son, had never run in the same circles at school. Nick was more scholastically minded, and Billy hung out with the hard-partying crowd. Where Nick went, Sarah went. Why hadn't it occurred to her during those years of innocence that there might have been a reason why she and Nick stuck so closely together?

She continued to admire the neatly trimmed shrubs, the bricks surrounding the flower beds, the trees, nicely mulched, that shaded the yard with spring green. Nick had begun earning money for college and med school in eighth grade by doing lawn care…and working on a wonderful tan and beautiful muscles that she was sure would've had most of the girls in their class following him around like hungry kittens if he'd ever gone without a shirt.

It was difficult for Sarah to decide if she felt more relieved or worried that Emma had spent the night under the Tyler roof—likely with her own father and grandfather, both oblivious. Family and old friends would surround Sarah and Emma here in Jolly Mill…if they stayed.

A dog barked from down the street, and a lawn-mower fired up a few blocks away—actually, in a town of eight hundred twelve people, there were only a few blocks in any direction. Sarah had loved growing up here. How she'd missed this place.

Focusing to keep her breaths steady, she marched to the front door and pressed the doorbell. The deep, soothing sounds of Westminster Abbey chimed through the house. She recalled those chimes from her earliest memories, and that soothed a little of her tension. Today was Saturday. Maybe everyone but Emma was sleeping in. Emma never slept in.

The door opened a crack, and dark brown, sleepy eyes peered out.

"Emma?"

The eyes widened and Emma gave a soft gasp as she pulled the door open. "Um, hi, sis. Wow, what're you doing here so early?"

Sarah stepped past the threshold. She grabbed Emma in a tight hug that obviously surprised Emma as much as it did her. "If you ever do anything like this again I'll ground you for the rest of your life. Do you know how scared I was?"

Emma held still for a moment, breathing slowly, as if soaking in the hug. They'd been close all of Emma's life, but because Mom and Dad were the disciplinarians, Sarah had always taken advantage of the opportunity to just enjoy time with her. She would need to start relying on her instincts as a kindergarten teacher when it came to discipline from now on. She could only imagine how Emma would respond to *that*.

Too soon for Sarah, her daughter wriggled free. "I told you where I was coming." She folded her arms across her underdeveloped chest. "Don't you think I'm old enough to take care of myself a few miles from home?"

"You drove across the whole lower state of Missouri! And don't think you're going to get away with this."

Emma sighed. "I know," she said in a singsong voice, "I'll have my cousin John to answer to when we get home."

"You'll have me to answer to, but the Tylers have been through too much already. They don't need two feuding sisters on their hands." It was a little late to start being the boss in Emma's life, but too often these past weeks she'd depended on John to step in as a father figure.

"According to Nick," Emma said, "when you and Shelby were together you were always feuding."

"Nick said that?"

"He even told me he had a crush on Shelby that lasted maybe a couple of weeks."

Sarah forgot to breathe for a moment. "He said that?" A couple of weeks?

"Okay, then he admitted maybe it lasted a little longer than that, but he wasn't in her league. He was a nerd, you know, not one of the jocks Shelby went for." She grinned up at Sarah. "Edward said you were Nick's true love, and everybody knew it."

Sarah tried not to react to that, but oh, it felt good to hear those words, whether or not they were true. And then she wondered why she felt so strongly about it after all these years.

"Y'all must've talked a lot last night." Sarah glanced up at the set of family photos to their left in the vestibule. One showed Nick at sixteen, standing above his seated parents. After all these years the memories tied knots around her heart. But before she could get maudlin she caught sight of a photo of Aunt Peg and Edward on their wedding day. Peg was what, twenty-four? Had Emma caught sight of herself in her grandmother's photo?

Emma closed her eyes with a sigh, and when she opened them again, they were slightly moist. "I'm sorry I scared you, sis, really. I couldn't stop thinking about that all the way here. I kept imagining how hurt you'd be, and I wanted to call you before I left, but really? Don't you want to know what happened to Mom and Dad?" Her typically soft, girlish voice tapered to a tiny tremble.

Sarah strolled past a padded foyer bench surrounded by a bentwood hall tree and an umbrella stand. She entered an open kitchen and living area that surely provided a pleasant great room for entertaining. She sank onto a pale green plush chair that faced an unobstructed view of the carefully tended backyard.

"I do want to know what happened to Mom and Dad," she said. "I also want to keep you safe. Nick's told me what he and his friend, the ex-cop, are doing, and I'm afraid we'll just get in the way."

Emma sat on the edge of a sofa that matched the chair, the sweet floral scent of her shampoo settling around them. "I'm not useless, you know. I can ask around. Besides, I want to get to know folks around here, and you can get reacquainted with old friends, right? What if Nick's right and someone can tell you something? Don't you want to know?"

Sarah suppressed a sigh. Her inquisitive, precious, irritating daughter. The trait of friendliness had been learned from the cradle. Sarah, on the other hand, would rather curl up for hours on her sofa in her tiny brick house at the edge of Sikeston, laptop across her knees as she compiled endless pages of fiction in her make-believe world with imaginary characters. For years she'd dreamed of having a novel published. It wasn't as easy as she'd once thought. With Mom and Dad gone, would she ever be able to return to that?

"Nick's really cool," Emma said. "So's Edward. We stayed up late last night and talked about Mom and Dad and Edward's wife."

"Aunt Peg."

"He said you and Shelby always called her that."

Emma reached over and touched Sarah's arm. "Please, please, don't you think we can stay awhile?"

Sarah braced herself against this child's well-known charm.

Emma turned and looked up at her, eyes large and entreating, a look Sarah had never been able to resist. "Did Nick tell you much about Gerard Vance?"

Sarah raised her eyebrows.

"The man who used to be a policeman down in Corpus Christi."

"He told me a little."

"He runs this homeless rehab place up at the top of the hills overlooking the mill. Isn't that really great?"

"Homeless rehab?"

"Yeah. The guy married an old friend of yours, Megan Bradley?"

"Megan? Really?" With a sense of loss, Sarah realized she had so much catching up to do. She'd missed nearly seventeen years' worth of Jolly Mill life.

"Yeah, she's a doctor now, and she met Gerard at his mission in Texas. He looks for people living on the street who want a new start in life, and he moves them to the rehab place. Just up that way on the hill." She pointed north. "He's helping Nick research the…the deaths." Her voice wobbled.

Sarah patted Emma's knee. "Sorry, sweetie. I'm so sorry. This is hard, I know." She blinked at the moisture that seemed so ever present in her own eyes the past three weeks. "Where are Nick and Edward now?"

Emma dabbed at her cheeks and sniffed. "Why do you call Edward by just his name when you always called his wife Aunt Peg?"

"Mom once told me it was a modified Southernism—instead of Miss Peg she was Auntie Peg, then the name shortened to Aunt when we got older. Edward insisted everyone call him Edward instead of Pastor or Reverend. He's kind of a laid-back guy."

"Edward said this is his only day to sleep late, so he'll be up later. I think I heard the shower a while ago, so that's probably Nick."

Then now would be her only chance to get Emma out of here. "Emma, honey, I know you don't want to think about it, but as I said, what if someone did cause those explosions? We could be in danger here, and Nick would be distracted if he has to see to our safety."

"But we can help. You're packing heat, aren't you?"

Sarah blinked. "You mean, did I bring my Smith & Wesson?" she asked dryly.

"In the wheel well, where you keep it? John told you to always keep it near you for protection. A woman alone can never be too—"

"Yes, but I don't ever want to have to use it, and it doesn't have to come to that if we would just leave."

"Nick got a couple more leads on his blog late last night," Emma said. "New person, fake name, couldn't trace it. Anyway, this person warned Nick to get on with his life if he wanted to keep it, and then they also mentioned how easily they could strike at any time. There was something about a party almost seventeen years ago?"

Sarah recoiled at the slap of those words. "The party?" So it was someone she'd known long ago. Someone, perhaps, who'd spiked the sodas at the going-away party Nora Thompson had thrown so the kids could say goodbye to Sarah's identical twin, Shelby—a party thrown at Shelby's request.

"Did Nick tell you about that?"

Emma shrugged. "He said someone spiked the soda. Edward said he thought the comment might be a prank. You know how sleazy people can get online."

"I doubt Nick's taking it casually. I'm not anymore." All the more reason to get Emma safely out of town.

"Why?"

"Honey, some jerk slipped a bunch of ecstasy into the sodas at that party, and the kids all kind of went nuts. Whoever sent that message to Nick obviously knew about it and is probably still in town."

Emma frowned up at her, scrunching her lips as she often did, which Mom had always warned her would give her wrinkles. "Edward would rather think it's some kind of hate crime. You know, like maybe somebody who hates Christians found out about the retreat. We hear a lot of stories about church shootings."

"But in Jolly Mill? This is the last place I can imagine that happening. Strangers couldn't even find it. This place is isolated. Besides, as Nick pointed out to me, if they wanted to kill a bunch of preachers they'd have struck earlier. I think this was more focused."

Emma took a shuddering breath, and Sarah wished she hadn't said that.

"Has Nick gathered any more information about the retreat center on Spring River that got shut down because of a dioxin spill?"

Emma slumped back into the cushions. "No, but he told me about it."

"So you can see why Dad might have been the one targeted. Hypothetically. He was instrumental not only in convincing the ministerial alliance to move their meeting place from Verona, but he spoke to others who met there, as well, and there was a general exodus."

"Nick's about to give up on that lead," Emma said. "Not much to go on, and as Edward said, who's going to wait more than thirty years to get their revenge? Nick made a few more calls last night. The retreat owner's wife got remarried and moved away with their daughter about a year after he killed himself. Two of his brothers stayed on and farmed and did pretty well. Gerard Vance?"

"The ex-cop, yes." Sarah smiled to herself. She could tell Emma was taken with Nick's friend. What impressed Sarah was that Megan Bradley had married him. She wondered, however, how Alec Thompson had taken that. Megan and Alec dated for a couple of years in high school. Of course, who knew about life in Jolly Mill after Sarah and her family moved away?

"Gerard had a talk with both of the brothers, and they said he always struggled with depression. They never blamed anything but that, and Gerard believes them."

"So Nick and Gerard are pursuing other leads?" Sarah asked.

"It's kind of hard to dig up dirt on a well-loved pastor." Never able to remain still for long, Emma sprang from the sofa and wandered through the room. "I drove through that town on my way here. Can you believe it's tinier than Jolly Mill?"

Sometimes her quick subject changes were dizzying, but Sarah kept up. Barely. "Verona? Why did you drive that route?"

"I wanted to drive past the plant that processed Agent Orange during the Vietnam War. That's, like, a gazillion years ago. That's what the dioxin leak was, you know."

"Emma, you went alone. At night."

"When you think about it, it's all kind of awful, huh?" Emma asked. "A tiny place in the middle of a peaceful farming community being used to make poison."

"Which part of this whole thing isn't awful?"

"Meeting Nick and Edward." Emma grinned, though it was a smile tinged by sorrow.

An unexpected chill breathed across Sarah's neck. Except for his temporary misadventures in English class—in which she tutored him—Nick was always brilliant, astute when it came to people. His initial hunch might have fizzled, and Sarah might just be allowing herself to be drawn into the drama, but she had always trusted his judgment.

Emma touched her arm. "Sis?"

Sarah allowed the warmth of that delicate hand to seep into her skin. "Yes."

"What's going on in your head? You look freaked."

"We need to go back to Sikeston. Today."

Emma jerked her hand away. "I didn't come all the way over here just to turn around and go back. I want to help—"

"How? It's sounding more and more as if someone intentionally killed our loved ones—there's probably someone in Jolly Mill we can't trust."

"Don't you want to see Edward again?"

"Of course I do." Part of her, however, felt desperate enough to want to take Emma right now and skip town before things could get out of hand completely, or before Emma impulsively stuck her nose where it didn't belong.

"We need to spend some time with him, Sarah, not just say hi and bye. He was one of Dad's best friends. Nick said Gerard is keeping watch from his place above town, where he has a clear view of all movement here in the valley, and besides, if we don't go see Carmen while we're this close she'll never forgive us. You want that on your conscience?"

What Sarah wanted was for her daughter to be safe. Yes, she wanted justice, but what were a rebellious teenager and a kindergarten teacher—who had, admittedly, been well taught by her policeman cousin to shoot a target—going to do to help catch killers? Another thing she didn't want was an emotional revelation that could have unbearable consequences—couldn't it?

"Well?" Emma demanded. "Do you?"

"We can see Carmen on our way out of town."

Emma crossed her arms again, her full lower lip jutting out in the tiny pout she often used to try to get her way—though she seldom succeeded, except with Sarah. "I'm staying."

This was not going well.

Nick scrubbed at his hair with the towel until both were equally damp and wondered if the friction of his movements might have scorched the terry cloth. He had blades to sharpen, lawns to mow and clients to placate, but right now all he wanted to do was pull on his clothes, go downstairs and wait for Sarah—she might even be here already. Was that the door chime he'd heard a few minutes ago while the shower was pounding his head, or was he imagining that? She'd sounded pretty wiped out last night, so she might have slept in this morning.

He flicked the towel over the bar, trying to breathe through the steamy air and thinking about last night's events. Emma was a good kid, as much as he could tell from a couple of hours of talk before they all retired. Immature, but what sixteen-year-old wasn't? She was a worker, that much he knew. He'd put her to work helping him load the pickup and trailer with his lawn-care equipment before Dad got home last night, and she'd volunteered to help him mow and trim today. Of course, he'd turned her down.

He was reaching for his T-shirt when a voice trailed from the other end of the hallway. He jerked, bumped his elbow on the towel rack and gritted back a growl.

The voice was Sarah's. He couldn't keep a smile from his face. She was here.

Then Emma's voice fell plaintively on his ears, not quite clear enough to make out the words. The voices grew softer but more intense, which meant they were probably arguing and didn't want anyone to hear. Which made him want to hear.

He took two seconds to comb his still-damp hair and cracked open the door. Time to calm the waters.

"…don't listen to me. You never listen! I told you, Nick said I could stay. We can both stay. Edward said so, too."

"And you thought you could accept the invitation for both of us without consulting me?"

"Come on, Sarah, they're family friends, practically family."

"You've been communicating with him online. Do you know how dangerous that could have been? What if it hadn't been Nick?"

"But it was."

"You didn't know that for sure. What would stop someone from contacting you online and posing as Nick to lure you down here? How did you know you weren't walking into a deadly trap?"

"But Nick said he wanted to talk to me…to us."

"He had no idea you were coming here. What you did was beyond dangerous."

The silence that followed her statement was telling. Nick waited for some exclamation of outrage from Emma, maybe a good, out-and-out catfight, but that wasn't Sarah's way except when it came to her twin, and judging by Emma's behavior last night, she might be impulsive but not aggressive.

"That car parked outside isn't yours," Sarah said at last. "The title reverted to me upon Mom's death, and I'm the one who calls the shots in our household now, whether we like it or not. That car goes back to Sikeston today, and you're driving it."

More silence.

Nick could almost close his eyes and picture the twins, Shelby and Sarah Russell, arguing in the school hallway, or on their front porch or just about anywhere. Typically it was Shelby who instigated the fight in an effort to force Sarah to do something she didn't want to do, such as join the cheerleading squad or go on a youth camping trip or sign up for summer sports. Sarah knew how to dig in and not be moved.

"I can't believe you would force me back home before I even have a chance to meet folks Mom and Dad used to know. How could you?"

It was time for Nick to make an appearance and stop eavesdropping. As the two continued to argue, he stepped down the hallway barefoot. He saw them before they knew he was there, saw Sarah's shiny, dark brown hair feathered around her face, those gray-green eyes that he used to look for in the school hallways. His friend. And when he wasn't being an idiot about her twin sister for those brief couple of weeks, he'd occasionally admitted to himself, even that long ago, that Sarah was the one with a special quality that put him at peace.

His breathing stopped for a second or two. Sarah's looks had changed dramatically, of course. Gone was the Goth look she'd worn to distinguish herself from her more popular sister. He still remembered the light of intelligence that had set off Sarah's gaze from Shelby's. Same coloring, different person looking out on the world, and that made all the difference.

"Sweetie, I'm not trying to be mean," Sarah said.

"If we go home we might never come back. I want to meet these people and get to know them." Emma marched across the living room to the sliding glass door that overlooked the backyard. Her warm brown eyes, that dark hair, the way she moved… Her appearance filled him with such curiosity. No one in the Russell family had brown eyes…did they?

"Now that we're here, Nick says we should be safe," Emma said. "Why can't we stay?"

"You're not calling the shots. I am." Sarah's voice held the barest thread of steel, tempered by gentleness.

Emma stood with her back to the room, arms crossed as she stared in the direction of the trees past the backyard.

"Do you know what people think when they see a girl your age drive up alone to a household of men?"

Emma turned around, rolling her eyes. "Oh, come on, Sarah." She held out her arms and looked down. "I could pass for twelve, and Edward's a pastor. He and Nick know everybody in town. Who's going to think something gross?"

"The smaller a town is, the more people notice."

Nick realized he was becoming an eavesdropper. "Trust me," he said at last, "most folks in this town know us better."

Sarah jumped to her feet and swung toward him, eyes wide. And then her full lips curved up in a smile of recognition. He remembered vividly the familiar light that had so often glowed from her when they were both young and full of life and ideas and dreams about the future.

Sarah's breath played and danced up and down her windpipe as she stared at Nicolas Tyler in his fully grown, fully masculine body, with shoulders appearing almost as wide as the swing set that they once played on in the Tyler backyard. His skin was already tanned, brown hair darkened by moisture from the shower. His dark brown eyes were still striated with flecks of sunshine gold. Emma's eyes. He entered the room in well-worn jeans and a navy T-shirt.

The impact after all these years took her breath completely.

His mouth curved up in a smile, setting off that characteristic cleft in his chin—the cleft his daughter had inherited. "Is this really Sarah Russell, who never stepped outside without her black everything?" Voice twice as deep as when they were teenagers, much nicer, even, than his phone voice. He sounded almost bemused.

Sarah chuckled. "Goth does not live on forever."

"I bet you were glad that spiderweb tattoo on your collarbone was temporary. And you finally dropped the face goo."

Sarah didn't blush easily, but she'd suddenly become Emma's age. "Hi, Nick." *Stop it, Sarah. It's no longer high school, and you're a grown woman.* "Thank you so much for calling me last night."

He glanced at Emma. Was he studying her features a little too carefully?

Emma looked away. "Sorry, sis, really. I should've called you. Nick and Edward both drilled me on it. Didn't mean to scare you."

"Why did you turn off your cell?"

Emma grimaced. "I forgot my charger. My phone went dead halfway here last night."

Something eased in Sarah's stomach. So Emma hadn't shut her out intentionally. Right? "It's a good thing I didn't know that last night when you were on the road alone. We'll have to hunt for it when we get home."

"But not today, right?" Emma gave Sarah her most plaintive look. "I know all about Dad's side of the family, but Mom had family here in Jolly Mill. I wanted to find out more about her, okay? Talk to people who knew her. You got to live here. I didn't. It's not fair."

"Fair? You grew up in Sikeston. Larger town,

more relatives, and they all knew Mom, too. We'll visit Carmen before we leave."

"I miss Mom and Dad." As more tears slid down Emma's face, Sarah sneaked at glance toward Nick's compassionate, sorrow-filled expression, and she knew all their lives had just taken a huge turn. He had questions; she could see them in his eyes. How was she going to answer them?

She was still lost in Nick's gaze when the sound of a softly closing door reached her. She glanced around the room. Emma was gone. Seconds later came the sound of the Beetle as it revved and buzzed away from the house. Emma was going to get her way, and nothing would ever be the same.

FOUR

Nick caught the flash of terror on Sarah's face when she realized Emma had slipped out. "That is one strong-willed kid."

Sarah reached for her purse. "Always has been. Got to stop her."

Nick placed a hand on her arm and felt that connection all the way to the pit of his stomach. Amazing how a simple touch could stir up so many memories…so much elation, so much loss.

"It's okay, Sarah. I'm sure she's just going to see Carmen. She and Dad talked about it last night, and he gave her directions to the clinic where Carmen works."

Sarah's muscles retained their tension.

"And you'd better believe Carmen's not going to let you out of town without a nice, long visit, anyway," he said. "The clinic's only a few blocks away. Emma's perfectly safe. She isn't six—she's sixteen."

"And what if the killer already knows who she is? Who I am? You know how quickly news spreads around here. If your friend Gerard is watching over the town with a telescope, why can't someone else?" Sarah took a tremulous breath and let him take her purse.

"Possible, but not probable. He has the highest vantage point." He could feel her quaver. "New at this mothering stuff, huh?"

Some of the tension eased from her face. "I'm not unfamiliar with the situation. That child is in her element with all this drama."

"She's a lot like Shelby sometimes, isn't she?"

Sarah's eyes widened and Nick wished he could read her mind. Once upon a time, he thought he could.

"This isn't the time for her to go traipsing off into unfamiliar territory," Sarah said.

"Dad showed her a map of Jolly Mill online last night." Nick placed her purse beside the overstuffed chair and gestured to her. "Sit for a minute. We can call the clinic and make sure Carmen's working the Saturday shift. She's usually there until noon. Emma wanted to see her first thing this morning." As he spoke, he picked up the phone on the end table and dialed. He could tell by the expression on Sarah's face that she wasn't inclined to sit still for long, but she sank onto the front edge of the cushion, shoulders straight, hands clasped on her lap, her delicate chin jutting out just a little. The expression in her gray-green eyes showed she was still braced for conflict. Like Nick, Sarah was at the end of her resources and was ready to jump at the slightest imagined threat. He could understand that so well.

"Edward? That you?" came Carmen's perky voice over the phone.

"Wrong Tyler," Nick said.

"Oopsie. Sorry, Nick. Everything okay? Nobody's sick, are they?"

"No. I actually called to talk to you. I don't suppose you've got company there now, have you? A red VW Beetle pulling up in the parking lot?"

There was a rustle of paper, a quick gasp and Carmen said, "Boy howdy, what d'you know? You clairvoyant or something?"

"It's your cousin Emma."

"Why, someone's getting out of the car now. Long, dark brown hair, a little skinny, but oh, how adorable. That's her, all right! Yee haw, but I'd've recognized that child anywhere, 'cept she almost looks like she's got some Tyler blood in her."

Hmm. "You don't say."

"When did she get to town?" There was the sound of quickened footsteps, as if Carmen might be running to the door to greet Emma.

"She arrived late last night. Sarah's here with me now." No need to go into detail yet. "With all that's happened, we can't take chances with Emma. Sarah didn't want her out on the streets by herself."

"You'll tell Sarah I want to see her, won't you?"

"She already knows."

"I feel awful for missing the funeral. I'd never have thought to see the day when Carmen Delaney would neglect family, but what with all the goings-on here—"

"Sarah understands how hard it was for all of us then. We'll be seeing you later, but once you get your visiting over with, would you send that child straight back here?" He'd found himself slipping back into old, casual, southern Missouri speech patterns since returning from Illinois.

"I'll be sure and tell her. Gotta go now, Nick. I see more folks pulling in. We've got a pretty full morning."

He said goodbye and disconnected. "Problem solved."

"For now." Sarah sounded resigned and still fearful. It was out of character for the Sarah Russell Nick had once known.

He sank onto the sofa armrest closest to her. "Coffee's brewed. Want some?"

She took a deep breath, as if enjoying the fragrance that wafted through the air. "Love some. Got cream?"

He smiled. "No sugar. Just like your dad used to drink his."

Her smile faltered only slightly, and then her attention shifted toward the hallway entrance. "Edward." She breathed the name, and her voice held a wealth of pain, love and something else.... Was it regret?

The man stood looking at her with tears in his eyes, then held out his arms. She jumped from her chair and rushed into them. Nick looked on as the two of them held on to one another, Dad in his fishing jeans and old, torn plaid shirt, his graying hair ruffled over his forehead. Sarah's profile showed such agony that Nick quietly turned and walked into the kitchen. Sarah needed a moment with Edward.

How could he have forgotten how close they were? Mom and Dad had loved both the twins, but Nick always suspected they held a special place in their hearts for Sarah, who soared above her sister in intelligence but floundered miserably trying to fit into any social mold.

His parents had always wanted him to have a baby sister. He'd overheard them talking about it one night when he was about seven. The doctor had broken the news to Mom that day that Nick was going to be an only child. Until then, he'd never thought about it much, but when his mother cried because she couldn't have another baby, he'd begun to pray that the doctors were wrong.

Though his prayers weren't answered, he imagined that the Russells had been deposited down the street just so they could share their very different twin girls with their best friends.

Nick took a tray from the cabinet above the coffeemaker and filled three mugs with coffee and cream. He added sugar for Dad, then slowly carried the tray back into the living room, where Dad and Sarah sat on the love seat, side by side, Dad with his arm around Sarah's shoulders. He gazed down at her as if soaking up her special presence.

"I didn't realize how much I needed to see you," Sarah told him softly. "You were like a second dad." Tears streamed down a face that Nick had seldom seen moist in all the years he'd known her.

"Still am, sweetheart," Dad said. "Let's make sure that doesn't change. I loved your folks as if they were siblings. So did your aunt Peg."

Sarah's face scrunched and she pressed her face into Dad's shirt. "And it all happened so quickly, all at once, and there was no time, and I couldn't be here for you, and—"

"And I couldn't be there for you." Dad's eyes were moist again, and then his face was wet, and he held Sarah in a tight embrace that spoke of his deep loss.

To the sound of Sarah's quiet sobs, Nick placed the tray on the coffee table and sank onto the chair across from them, giving them time and silence to seek solace in one another as he shared their pain. Not for the first time, he felt a secret rush of gratitude that Emma's headstrong deliberation had brought the Russell girls across the state, despite the danger that could have posed. When it was time for them to return home, he would go along to make sure they stayed safe.

If his guess was correct, Dad would go, too. He only hoped that wouldn't be for a few days. Nick had already called Gerard this morning, had alerted several old hunting buddies—those who knew how to handle a weapon responsibly—and though Jolly Mill didn't have police coverage, they definitely had watchmen guarding them from nearly every block in town, and several around the outer edges. The sheriff's office in Neosho wasn't convinced that there was a serial killer in Jolly Mill, but the residents were.

Even more protective than the actual weapons was the fact that word was spreading about the community circling the wagons and watching out for one another. If a killer was still in town, that person must be lying low.

Nick pulled tissues from a decorative box on the side table. He silently thanked God for the solidarity of friends and vowed to apologize for his reticence since arriving here. He'd been devastated, bitter, lost when he came home from Illinois to find his father so broken. Old friends had called, but he hadn't returned their calls. They had surrounded him and Dad at Mom's funeral, sent cards and flowers— but mostly they brought food to fill the freezer to keep two bachelors from starving. Emma's arrival last night, and Sarah's this morning, had changed things for him.

He squished a tissue in his hand as he thought about his actions the past three weeks, then looked up to find Dad and Sarah watching him. He gave them each a tissue and then handed Dad his coffee.

"Sugar?" Dad mopped his face.

Nick nodded, cleared his throat, gave Sarah a mug of her own.

She thanked him and took a hearty sip, then placed the mug down and dabbed at her eyes and nose. "I didn't mean to cause all this." Her voice wobbled as it had last night on the phone.

"You didn't mean to bring comfort to two people starving for it?" Nick asked.

She acknowledged his statement with a nod and accepted another tissue. It, too, became soaked. With a sigh, she took another swallow of coffee, then closed her eyes and leaned back. "This is delicious. Real cream."

"From a church member up the creek a ways," Dad said. "He keeps us in milk and cream from his dairy. Where'd Emma get off to?"

Sarah gave Nick a look. "Last I heard, she was at the clinic."

"Oh, good. Carmen will keep an eye on her."

"I'm sure Carmen has a busy schedule today," Sarah said. "I should probably take a stroll down there and make sure Emma doesn't make a pest of herself or take off for some other part of town."

Dad laid a hand on Sarah's arm. "Take a break from your mothering duties for a little while. Please tell me you and Emma will stay in Jolly Mill for a few days. Your aunt Peg loved you so much. Having you here would bring me a lot of comfort. I think, despite our fears, you might find some comfort here, as well."

Nick saw the hesitation in her eyes. She glanced toward the vestibule, her gaze seeming to rest on the large family portrait that hung above a sofa table. She blinked, swallowed and took a deep breath.

Sarah managed to set her mug down without spilling a drop of coffee. It wasn't easy. She met Nick's gaze, and though she saw lingering sadness there, she also saw an impish mischief. She might be able to put her foot down with him, and even with Emma, but she could never tell Edward no.

Besides, being held in Edward's arms had reattached the emotional umbilical cord she'd once had to this home.

The Tylers had kept an open-door policy for the kids from church. Though Shelby spent time here with the rest of her friends, Sarah had her own special time alone with Edward and Aunt Peg, and often Nick, when Shelby was away at games. Mom and Dad almost always attended those games. That was when Sarah felt as if she blossomed under the loving, individual attention of the Tylers.

"Tell me you at least packed a suitcase," Nick said, placing his empty mug on the tray.

"I did. I can't tell you for sure what's in it. I wasn't thinking clearly when—"

"I'll bring it in."

She met his gaze, silently begging him not to push her further. "I do want to stay for a while," she admitted. "But maybe I should make arrangements with Carmen. I don't want the rumor mill to hurt your—"

"I'm not worried about the rumor mill," Edward said gently.

"Neither am I," Nick said, still watching her closely. "But judging by the way Carmen talked this morning, Dad, I'm afraid she might pack up and move in, too, if Sarah and Emma decide to stay here."

Edward gave a soft chuckle. "You could be right, and having Carmen move in might raise a few eyebrows, especially with those who know we dated in high school." He patted Sarah's hand. "You do realize how badly we felt when no one was able to make it to Sikeston. Carmen was beside herself."

Sarah nodded. "The Russell clan packed the funeral home, so don't worry, we had support." In fact, she'd been overwhelmed by the crush of people when all she'd wanted to do was hide away.

"Now that Emma's met Carmen," Nick said, "I'm sure she'll be eager to stay with her."

"Have you heard anything more this morning about Chaz?" Edward asked his son.

"I talked to his mother earlier. I think she's convinced her son was simply frightened and left. He did pack some clothing, and he'd warned her not to talk about the explosions to anyone."

"But he didn't say why?" Sarah asked.

"He's young," Edward said. "Too inexperienced for the responsibility laid on him. This town's filled with good folk, but every place has a troublemaker or two, and our kind of tragedy could have sparked an ornery streak in someone."

"I would have thought that, too, Dad." Nick's voice was gentle. "If it wasn't for the same thing happening in two places." It sounded as if they'd debated this subject a few times already, and Edward still hovered between belief in Nick's suspicions and hope that the explosions were simply catastrophic coincidences.

Sarah picked up her mug and swallowed the final drops of coffee. "I think I should go rescue Carmen from Emma so she can get her work done." She reached for her purse. "I'll see if Carmen's up for some overnight company."

Nick stood with her. "No need for you to go alone. Dad? Want to join us?"

Edward held out his arms, his holey old shirt evidence that he had other plans. "Fishing. Supposed to meet Chapman down at the bridge in a few minutes, and I've already stood him up twice. That guy thinks fishing can heal anything." He leaned over Sarah and kissed the top of her head. "I'll be seeing you later, right?"

"Yes, Edward." Whatever came of this trip, she knew she couldn't leave yet. It was why she'd been so afraid to come in the first place. One didn't just return to the place she'd always called home in her heart, then up and leave without some reconnection. Right now, however, remembering Mom and Dad as they were, and being reminded so forcefully of their deaths, was too much to handle. She needed time alone to digest this sudden turn of events.

She looked up at Nick. "Don't you have work to do? I saw the lawn equipment loaded in that truck with your name on the side. Though last I'd heard you were a doctor practicing in Rockford, Illinois."

"Long story."

"You don't have to explain anything to me."

Nick nodded toward the kitchen. "Coffee to go?"

"I'm fine."

He rested a hand on her shoulder. "Then let's take a stroll to the clinic."

All it took was that touch, and Sarah suddenly didn't care that she wouldn't have time alone. She'd been alone for far too long, come to think of it. She gave Edward another hug and stepped out the door Nick held for her.

She caught another whiff of the breakfast smells from down the street. A sense of long-ago loss caught her in its grip as she recalled leaving this home she'd known for sixteen years.

"Does your uncle still run the best diner in town?"

"No. Billy took Parker's over a few years ago."

"And it didn't go under?"

"Hasn't yet. Uncle Will talked quite a bit about deeding the restaurant to Mom."

"I bet Billy hated that." The sight of Billy Parker managing a restaurant would be a new experience. In school he'd barely attended class enough to pass, and that was in a haze of pot smoke.

"You could say that. I was dumb enough to tease one day that Billy was the reason Alec Thompson decided to build the clinic." Nick strolled along beside her, hands in his hip pockets. "What with the impending food poisoning epidemic we were all sure would kill the town."

She chuckled. Nick and Billy were polar opposites.

"He kicked me out of the restaurant."

Sarah laughed out loud. "Served you right."

"There it is," he said, nudging her with his elbow. "I knew you had it in you. Remember that one place in the cavern where our voices echoed a half dozen times?"

"Two times. They echoed twice. You always exaggerated."

"Except when you laughed. Then it seemed to go on forever."

She couldn't help noticing that her steps grew slower, and that Nick's matched hers. The sun had barely begun to warm the morning air, and it sounded as if every bird in the sky celebrated the warmth after an extra-cold winter.

It wasn't until Nick and Sarah had reached a familiar corner that she realized they would be passing the home where she grew up, a little brick house where she and Shelby had shared a bedroom until they were twelve. A church member had turned the back porch into a third bedroom for Sarah before she and Shelby grew old enough to strangle each other. Her parents had probably tired of being kept awake when their daughters were in the mood to argue.

She smiled at the thought. They hadn't always bickered. In fact, plunged back in time by visual memories, she had greater clarity about it. She and Shelby had chattered and laughed more often than they argued. It was only during those times when Shelby insisted that Sarah do something she didn't want to do that their fights got bad; Sarah never gave in, and Shelby never gave up.

"Memories?" Nick asked.

Sarah kicked at a tuft of clover that forced its way through a crack in the sidewalk. "I was just thinking how relieved my parents must have been after they had that third bedroom built. When Shelby and I were together we were sometimes rowdy."

"That's because you were so different."

Sarah's steps slowed. She gave Nick a sidewise glance. "You do realize, don't you, that the whole reason for that Goth chick getup of mine was because I got so sick of people telling us how alike we were."

He drew a little closer to her side. "The only people who believed that didn't know you." He reached out and tugged at a short strand of her layered hair. "Your parents never told you how alike you were, did they?"

"Mom dressed us in the same outfits when we were little."

"I'm sure it was less expensive and faster that way, but that's probably the only reason anyone ever compared you and Shelby. I never had trouble telling you two apart."

Sarah gently pressed her teeth into her lower lip. How wrong he was…at least about that one time… "Shelby was the outgoing, friendly—"

"Shelby's the extrovert—you're the thoughtful one. It's always been that way. Shelby's thoughts pretty much slipped out of her mouth before they went through any kind of process inside the skull. It was as if she actually couldn't make sense of them unless she could first share them with others—usually you."

"That's how you could tell us apart? Before my Goth phase, that is."

He shrugged. "You know, windows to the soul and all that. Shelby's eyes and face were always in motion. She was always looking for someone to talk to even if she wasn't talking at the moment. She had a habit of looking through me, which made it easy to observe her."

Without thinking, Sarah reached out and caught his hand. "I'm sorry."

He squeezed back. "I'm not. Now you, on the other hand, were the opposite. Instead of seeking out people who might become a part of an entourage of friends, you chose wisely and permanently, and you kept only a few of the best people with the best qualities."

"You, for instance."

He grinned at her. She could lose herself in this man.

"I'm sure the move was hardest on you," he said.

She liked that he continued to hold her hand. Of course, it wasn't an intimate gesture, it was simply a warm connection of old friends. Right?

"Did Shelby thrive in St. Louis?" he asked.

Sarah released his hand and reached up to shove away hair that had blown across her face in the gentle morning breeze. Even in her absence, Shelby was the topic of conversation, it seemed. "You know how larger schools are. They can be overwhelming."

"Don't tell me she didn't get top pick for cheerleader."

"She didn't try." Sarah closed her eyes briefly, recalling Shelby's mortification and anger when it became evident that Sarah was with child. She'd accused Mom and Dad of leaving Jolly Mill to protect Sarah and their own reputations. The unfairness of her accusation became obvious when Emma was born almost exactly nine months after the night of the party.

"Everyone in Jolly Mill was surprised to hear of Emma's birth." Nick's voice seemed to grow quieter, and something about it put Sarah on edge.

She silently begged him not to ask for details. "A few months after she was born, Dad decided hospital chaplaincy wasn't for him. He started looking for a church to pastor in Sikeston, which was only a couple of hours' drive from where we lived at the time. Counting first, second and third cousins once, twice and thrice removed, the Russells pretty much make up a sizable portion of the city of Sikeston."

When they reached the far end of the yard, Sarah glanced toward her old bedroom. Had that bedroom not been built, Emma might not have been conceived. It had been much easier to sneak out the back, all decked out like Shelby—no one had really expected Sarah to attend anyway, had they? "I was stunned to discover that I missed Shelby when we had separate rooms."

"I'm sure you miss her now."

Sarah glanced up at him. Was this a moment for honesty, or should she just gloss over his statement? Though Shelby loved Emma, she had obviously never forgiven Sarah for her pregnancy. That was strange, too, because Shelby had volunteered at a shelter for unwed mothers before she married and took off for Africa. Naturally, she would have had high expectations for her own sister, the daughter of a pastor, but wasn't her judgmental spirit also wrong? She knew as well as the rest of the family about the night of Emma's conception, about the spiked sodas.

"I changed when we left here," Sarah said, instead of responding to his observation. "In fact, I was homeschooled in St. Louis because I couldn't face the crush of huge classes and crowded hallways, teachers who didn't know me and never would." And of course, the growing child inside her would have drawn a lot of attention. Mom and Dad had given her great compassion while Shelby barely spoke to her. Sarah had been left with no doubt about who would be raising her baby—her parents. They made it clear the moment Emma was born that they loved her as their own.

"I changed, too," Nick said. "When you left here."

She looked up at him and studied the strong lines of his face, the eyes that seemed to have darkened to teak in the past few moments. She refused to play the old silent game she'd played with herself as they traveled across the state to St. Louis: Which twin did he miss the most?

"How did you change?" she asked.

"I realized I'd lost my best friend."

A warm awareness spread through her. Shelby had never been his best friend. "Me, too."

"I remember the day your family loaded the last of your belongings into your big old Buick and your dad was ready to drive away," Nick said.

"I ran to your house."

"You were out of breath when you got there, crying, with all that black makeup streaking down your white face. You were a mess."

"Aunt Peg held me and let me cry, and she didn't care if I got all that nasty face stuff on her shirt."

"She cried, too, if I remember correctly," Nick said. "Dad and I would have joined you, but you know men. We just stood there and looked stupid and cleared our throats a lot."

"It was the worst day of my life until three weeks ago."

"I remember it well."

"You say you changed?" She cast another glance over her shoulder toward the house where she'd grown up.

"I realized I'd become too complacent. Because I'd had a buddy—" He nudged her with his elbow. "That would be you, by the way, and I sort of counted on you more than I thought. And then you were gone. I never was the life of the party, was pretty much a science nerd. I guess if I'd dyed my hair black and borrowed your eye stuff, I'd have been as Goth as you."

"You hated my Goth phase."

"Only because it covered who you really were. Anyway, I buried myself in study, got a scholarship, got another scholarship, finished med school at Columbia and never learned how to choose the right friends. At least, not of the female persuasion."

"But you got married."

"One would think that a guy who graduated top of his class in med school would have the wisdom to make better choices."

"Remember we studied that? Intelligence quotient does not necessarily equal common sense. That was my area of expertise. You should've called me when you went looking for that special someone. I could have helped you with that."

His footsteps slowed. "If you'd still been in my life I wouldn't have needed the help," he said quietly.

The warmth inside her deepened.

"There's the clinic." He pointed to a long antiqued brick building a block away to the left of the street.

"And the parking lot," he said. "And I hate to say this, but I don't see a little red VW anywhere."

Sarah tripped on the edge of the blacktop and gasped. Nick caught her. "She's gone?"

FIVE

Nick felt the contagion of Sarah's alarm as he rushed with her across the street. He led her through the wide grassy verge to the parking lot, a dozen thoughts shooting through his mind, none good. His suspicions had obviously affected her, and he was sorry for it, but hard as he tried, he couldn't convince himself they were overreacting. Carmen had said she wouldn't let Emma leave, but Carmen didn't know Emma the way he was beginning to know her. If Emma decided to do something, she didn't wait for permission.

What if Sarah was right? Word spread quickly here, and he didn't doubt word had spread about the presence of Emma—the daughter of two people caught in an explosion, possibly murdered. Was a killer set on revenge? Would a killer also set sights on the daughter of those victims?

Sarah caught up with him when he reached the front door of the clinic. "She didn't pass us on her way back to the house. Was the conference center on the map Edward gave her?"

"No, the map ends at Capps Creek, and we didn't give her directions."

"She could stop and ask anyone on the street."

He was beginning to realize he should've never talked Sarah into waiting. "Keeping up with her must be like keeping up with an oversize toddler."

Sarah glanced at the patients in the waiting room and leaned closer to Nick. "Emma takes people by surprise on occasion," she said more quietly. "She's always been full of energy and curiosity, but now there's more of an edge to her."

Nick led Sarah to the closed glass reception window, where Carmen was bent over pulling files from a drawer.

As usual, Carmen wore her brightly colored scrubs—this time pink with lifelike bunny faces on her shirt. When she looked up, her green eyes widened and her typical grin spread across her face. Running a hand through newly short, perky blond hair that took ten years from her face, she turned and rushed through an open threshold. Seconds later she opened the large door that led back to the treatment rooms.

"Sarah Russell—that you, girl?" Without waiting for an answer she held her arms out wide and enveloped Sarah in a hug.

Sarah returned the affection in full force, and for

a moment, watching her, Nick thought she might once again burst into sobs. All Nick wanted to do right now was find Emma, and he couldn't help wondering at this sudden osmosis between himself and Sarah. He didn't even have to look at her to feel her tension and fear battling the heightened emotions over seeing Carmen after so many years.

Sarah released her cousin. "Carmen, I never realized how much you looked like Mom." There was a catch in her voice. "We thought Emma was here."

Carmen reached for a tissue and dabbed at her eyes, and gave one to Sarah as she drew them into the staff break room for some privacy. "Here you go, honey. We started running low on them so I bought a case last week. Everyone's been so upset about our losses, it seems the whole town's swimming in tears. I need to start using paper towels to mop up this mess of a face. Emma and I cried up a storm."

Sarah held up a hand that successfully stopped Carmen's flow of words. "Emma."

"I'm surprised you didn't see her. She left a few minutes ago."

"She didn't come back to the house," Nick said.

"Uh-oh. You think she went to Parker's? Poor kid's stomach was rumbling so loudly I thought there might be a bear in the waiting room. She said she needed some breakfast. Too bad she didn't wait just a couple more minutes, 'cause Nora dropped off goodies about the time Emma pulled out. Not that they're nutritious goodies, but they'd fill her stomach. I was about to call you at the house and make sure she got there."

Nick looked at Sarah. "Parker's. Dad told her about their cinnamon rolls last night." He couldn't help wondering, as he always did, how Carmen could say so much so quickly without taking a breath. It was a gift. Of sorts.

"She told me she got lost finding town last night and she's afraid to wander too far away," Carmen said. "But no way she'd get lost between here and Parker's."

"Emma's kind of a wild card," Nick said. "We don't want to take the chance of the wrong person getting close to her. She wants to get to the bottom of her parents' deaths, and she apparently sees herself as some kind of super heroine."

Carmen grimaced. "Comes from her mother's side of the family."

"It may just be fear talking," Sarah said, "but I need to find her, if only for my peace of mind."

"Oh, honey, I'm so sorry. Of course y'all are distraught. Why didn't I think? I know what you need to do, though. You and Emma need to mingle a little, let our home folks know who she is. They'll recognize you, of course, but they need to know to watch out for Emma if she's going to be tooling around town like this."

"I think that's what she plans to do," Nick said.

Carmen opened a cabinet door, pulled out a purse and removed a set of keys. She shook her head and held the keys out for Nick. "I tend to agree with Edward about those explosions—just can't quite wrap my head around somebody from here actually doing the deed—but of course you're going to worry. Go find that girl. I know you walked here, because I saw you two coming down the street, talking and laughing like a couple of old friends. Take my gas guzzler. That ol' truck's got pipes as loud as a train engine, but it'll get you through town and to the right place."

When Nick hesitated, Carmen pressed them into his hand. "If you're that worried about her, you'd better take what you can get right now." She patted his arm and pointed out the window toward a white pickup truck with pink detailing and seating for five.

She walked with them down the hallway of the clinic and out the front door. Before they could leave, however, Carmen caught Sarah by the arm. "You and Emma are staying with me, of course."

"Nick said you have an alarm system."

"Sure do, state of the art, put in by our own ex-cop, Gerard Vance." She grinned. "Oh, and I must also mention I've got my sweet bodyguard at the house—Nina."

"You never told me about a bodyguard," Nick said.

"Well, young man, you don't get down here too

often, do you? Haven't even been to my house since you got back, and you haven't asked how I stay in shape lately, despite the dangerous treats Nora keeps foisting on us." Carmen raised her arm to show a muscle. "Not many women my age can brag about that. Nina's the mutt I rescued from a pound last year. I think she's mostly Doberman. I'd advise you to wait until I'm off at noon to move your luggage into my house. You'll need an introduction. Think you'll feel safe enough with all that protection, Sarah?"

"I'm not sure I'll feel safe anywhere right now."

"Then you might as well be with friends and family."

Nick edged his way closer to Carmen's truck.

"My house is safe," Carmen said. "Or if you prefer I could pack a bag and camp out on Edward's living room sofa." She leaned close and winked. "That'd start a nice, fun little rumor for Jolly Mill residents to sink their teeth into, wouldn't it?"

Sarah gave her cousin a final hug. "I'd better go before Nick takes off without me."

"Oh, Sarah, you let your ol' cuz teach you a few things about men while you're here. There's no threat of him taking off without you, my dear. Trust me."

"Carmen," Nick called over his shoulder. "I'm thirty feet away. I can hear you."

Carmen chuckled and slapped Sarah on the shoulder. "We'll talk later."

Sarah slid into the passenger side of the pickup and buckled up, obviously not willing to make eye contact with Nick. Her cheeks were slightly pink. "Off to Parker's?"

"You can smell Billy's smoked, greasy meats all over town on Saturday morning, which is the only reason his business is still booming years after Uncle Will retired to Florida. I'm surprised half the town hasn't dropped dead of heart attacks."

"I thought you said Emma'd be safe with Carmen."

"Yes, I did say that, didn't I?" He glanced at Sarah, who sat facing straight ahead, shoulders stiff, gripping her hands together in her lap so hard her fingertips were white. "If we do find the Beetle at Parker's, will you try to calm down just a little?"

She looked up at him, and he could read a soul-deep vulnerability in her eyes.

"Remember what I told you last night? You're not alone, Sarah."

"She's my responsibility, and I know how impulsive she can be. Maybe I'm overreacting, but I can't take any chances with her."

"I'm catching on pretty quickly to her tactics. Let me take some of this load, okay? You won't be any good to yourself or Emma if you give in to panic." He placed a hand over hers.

Sarah felt the warmth of Nick's hand melting into her icy fingers. She hadn't realized how tightly she was wound. She focused on releasing some of the tension, flexing her shoulders, scooting more deeply into the seat, and was glad the truck didn't have a manual shift, because that allowed Nick to keep his hand on hers long enough for her to release at least a little of the stiffness in her grip as he drove from the clinic lot.

"Since I attended med school in Missouri, I have a license to practice medicine here," Nick said. "I'm going to do that right now. From what I've seen, and from what I've experienced, myself, I'm diagnosing you with PTSD."

She shook her head. "I can handle this."

"You lost both your parents and suddenly became the guardian of a very headstrong teenager who also, most likely, has PTSD mingling with grief after discovering their deaths might have been murder. You tell me if you aren't experiencing some symptoms of PTSD."

"Enough with the poor-little-Sarah routine, okay? You're doing what you need to. Maybe I do have PTSD, but I'll deal with it."

Nick removed his hand so he could pull into a slot down the street from Parker's, which was practically surrounded by automobiles this time of morning—and one of those cars was a red VW.

The relief that rushed through Sarah made her light-headed. She opened her door and slid out. "Time to drag our wanderer back with us."

He joined her. "Or we could just sit with her and share her breakfast."

"Not me, thank you. Her thing for breakfast is green smoothies. Does Parker's serve green smoothies?"

"You're not going to believe this, but yes. Some of the ladies of the town ganged up on my poor cousin a few months ago, apparently, and told him they would no longer eat here if he didn't start preparing some healthier fare. Remember Petra Journigan? She came to our school her sophomore year, when we were seniors. Red hair, freckles, friendly."

"Dated Billy for a while, but had a huge crush on you?"

Nick looked askance at Sarah. "No way."

"She did—I could tell. Girls see things guys like you never see." Such as how much his best friend adored him.

"If you say so. Anyway, she left after graduation, then a few months ago she came back to Jolly Mill and got a job at Parker's. Best cook he's ever had."

"Is she dating him again?"

"Nope. She's seeing Alec Thompson. Anyway, she experimented with some smoothie recipes and Parker's now has a booming business with the health nuts in town, and in Pierce City and Monett. Carmen claims to have lost twenty pounds because of those smoothies."

"I thought she attributed that to her dog, Nina.

Am I confusing Petra with someone else, or was she the one who came to school with bruises? I used to see them when we dressed for PE."

"I heard rumors. I think Dad had a talk with the family, though he never mentioned it to me. I followed him one day when he went to their house, and for a while things seemed better in the rumor mills. She was sure in a hurry to leave after graduation, though. Now she's creating new dishes and catering for Parker's, so she did something constructive since graduating."

He opened the squeaky front door and held it for Sarah while the scents of smoked meats, freshly brewed coffee and maple syrup wafted from the huge dining area. Sarah's stomach rumbled almost loudly enough to be heard above the chatter of a couple dozen diners. How could someone walk into this place and be accosted by such wonderful aromas, then settle for a thick, green swallow of sludge?

"Sarah Russell!" called a handsome man from a table by the coffee bar.

Sarah recognized Alec Thompson immediately. Everyone would know Alec, since he and his mother, Nora, owned multiple businesses in Jolly Mill. His sandy-brown hair was shorter than she remembered, his eyes just as dark as those of his mother, and just as filled with intelligence. But as he left his table to greet them, Sarah searched the crowded room for Emma. And didn't see her.

She accepted Alec's quick hug, warm greeting and commiseration about her loss, while feeling that insistent worry return.

"Alec, good to see you again." Nick placed a hand on Sarah's shoulder and squeezed. "We could use your help. You see that red VW out there?"

Alec nodded. "Sure did. A sweet young thing climbed out of it, didn't even look old enough to drive, and came in here, ordered a smoothie to go, paid for it and left. She took off walking with her smoothie. Someone said they saw the VW at your house early this morning."

"That's right."

"She a visiting relative of yours, Nick? Because I could've sworn she looked just like your mama's school picture hanging in the high school upper hallway."

There was just the briefest of hesitations before Nick said, "She's Emma Russell, Sarah's baby sister."

"You don't say." Alec gave Sarah a long, astute appraisal, then turned narrowed eyes to Nick. "And all the time I watched her I was thinking how much she looked like a Tyler."

Sarah swallowed hard. She could feel the men's attention on her. "H-how long ago did you say she left Parker's?"

Alec glanced at his watch. "Oh, I'd say no more than fifteen minutes. What's Shelby up to these days?"

"Feeding the hungry in Tanzania. Please, Alec, could you tell us which direction Emma went? It's urgent."

"Oh, sure. I'm sorry. She headed east along the sidewalk, but—"

"Thanks. I think I'll head that way."

Nick placed an arm around her shoulders, slowing her exit. "Did she talk to anyone while she was here?" he asked Alec. "She's the girl who made comments on the blog."

Alec frowned. "That was her? Did you read those threats someone posted? Somebody's nervous. I tried to track them online but couldn't get anywhere. You?"

Sarah tried to tug away from Nick's grasp. He held her more firmly.

"Alec, we don't feel safe having Emma traipsing all over town by herself."

Alec held his hand up. "Of course. Sorry, my brain's not all there today. Just a sec." He turned and spoke to a server about his order, then walked over and chatted with the cashier as he paid her.

Sarah's cell phone buzzed from her pocket. She jerked it out and saw her cousin's caller ID. "John?"

"Got something for you, cuz, and you're not going to like it."

Sarah bit her lip.

"Soon as I got to the station this morning I called

a buddy I met last year at a state training course. He's working with the sheriff over there in Newton County now. They're in the process of contacting the family of a Mr. Charles Collins. Some fishermen found his body early this morning north of I-44 in Spring River."

Sarah sucked in her breath. "His body?" She looked up at Nick. "He drowned?"

"No news on that yet for sure, but there weren't any obvious marks on him. Highway patrol found his car upriver, where he had apparently missed a bridge and flown his car into the water. There was broken glass on the road, and the rear end of his car was damaged."

"Oh, John, they can't say that was an accident." She was going to be sick. She was going to faint. Nick caught her against him, then eased her into a chair. He reached for the phone.

She shook her head. "John, they called him Chaz. He was the inspector for the explosions, and he was removed from the case after he got some facts messed up."

There was a heavy sigh over the line. "I'll talk to my captain. He's got contacts all over the state— you know what a small world policing is in southern Missouri. Meanwhile, you need to keep Emma under surveillance."

"I will when I find her."

His alarm pounded through the silence.

"I've got help," she said. "We'll find her."

"I'm getting time off and—"

"No. Stay in Sikeston. You don't have any authority here."

"But Newton County has an overworked sheriff's department, and Jolly Mill is too tiny to get a lot of attention."

"Nick has a friend who's an ex-cop. Three-fourths of the population here can handle a weapon if need be. My old hometown's pretty close-knit."

"Then stick to Nick like tar. If someone followed this poor Chaz, you could just as easily be followed wherever you go."

She wished he hadn't said that.

"Something's up, Sarah. People you loved were up to their necks in it, whether they knew it or not. Let's just hope Nick and his friends figure out what that is before anything else happens."

Sarah's eyes slid shut. "Thanks, John. Emma can't be too far away."

"Would you at least call me and let me know when you find her?"

"Of course." She saw Alec turn away from the cash register. "Gotta go."

After she disconnected, she looked up at Nick and shook her head.

Alec walked back toward them with a bag, chuckling from his talk with the cashier until he saw Sarah's face. He sobered. "What's wrong?"

"Chaz Cooper was found dead in Spring River," she said.

Alec fumbled his take-out bag. "When?"

"Earlier this morning. I don't know if the sheriff's told the family yet. My cousin's a police officer in Sikeston, so he's trying to keep up with me and keep me updated."

"How was Chaz found?" Alec asked.

She gave the men the details, then walked out the front door. She knew the place where Chaz had gone into the river. Barely twenty miles north of Jolly Mill, it was near a wilderness area where Dad used to take her hiking when Shelby was busy with school activities.

"No way is that a coincidence," Nick said, joining her on the sidewalk.

"That's why I have to find Emma." She turned and gazed across Capps Creek, the banks of which were about a hundred yards from them across the street. Behind the creek rose the cliffs on which the conference center had rested for decades, hidden by the trees. The only building she could see now was once a resort.

"Is that the rehab center you told me about?" she asked Nick.

"That's it, and see that glassed-in deck?" He

waved toward the building that seemed to float above the trees from their vantage point. "Gerard's probably wielding his telescope."

Alec stepped outside. "You're telling me someone wanted so badly to shut Chaz up they hunted him down and ran him off the bridge?"

"What does it sound like to you?" she asked. "But keep it quiet. We don't want the whole town finding out about it before the family does."

"At least the sheriff's office will have to get involved," Nick said.

"Don't get your hopes up," Alec said. "They're still dealing with budget cuts, and they have plenty more populated areas to patrol. We have to find Emma and wrangle that little filly into a corral. She's out of control."

"What did you find out about her visit in the diner this morning?" Nick asked.

"Emma asked Carol about the explosions, and though Carol warned her not to get close to those places, she did tell her where they happened."

"That's where she's headed, then," Sarah said.

"Let's go see what we can find." Alec led the way, and Sarah was reminded of his take-charge tendencies, much like his mother, Nora. He didn't take the time to stow his breakfast in his car, but marched so quickly down the street Sarah had to rush to keep up with him and Nick.

There was no longer a bit of doubt in Sarah's

mind. None of the deaths had been accidents. There had been a murderer among them. Whether or not there still was was anyone's guess.

SIX

Since Nick had last visited the mill park, the citizens of Jolly Mill had worked hard to make the creek side a beautiful place for community gatherings. A wooden archway served as an entry into the flower-strewn grass with a paved walkway. Had he not been so anxious to find Emma, he would have paused to admire the flowers that bloomed everywhere.

Without stopping, Alec yanked a breakfast sandwich from his bag, tossed his trash in a receptacle near the entryway and led them through the arch. He glanced over his shoulder at Nick. "If you two want to head toward the old bridge, I'll take the new one that leads into the new subdivision and the rehab center."

"The new bridge is closer to both places," Nick said. "We could all go that way."

"Does Emma know that?"

"Probably not," Sarah said. "She never takes time to ask for detailed directions."

"Then we should separate." Alec unwrapped his

sandwich. "If I find her first I'll haul her down the hill over my shoulder if I have to, but if she went the other way we might miss her."

"Fine, give us your cell number," Nick said, "and I'll give you mine."

"Yours is never on. Do you know how many times I've tried to call you?"

"It's on today. And since you're going up to the rehab center first, why don't you grab Gerard on your way? He can help look."

Alec hesitated. His lip curled just enough to give away his thoughts. "Your cell's on, you call him."

So that was the situation. Alec had never trusted newcomers, and he had a special reason to dislike Gerard; not only was the ex-cop now married to Alec's clinic doctor, whom Alec had dated in high school for two years, but Alec likely perceived Gerard's rehab center as a threat to the town's job market and security.

"We need his help," Nick said.

"He's good with a gun, I'll give him that," Alec said. "And that little gal could end up anywhere."

"As if you know what to expect from her," Sarah said.

Alec winked and grinned at her. "That's because I knew her...sisters." Again, that quizzical gaze that had obviously made Sarah uneasy in the diner.

"So you'll get Gerard?" Nick asked.

"If you'll consider working for me at the clinic, should we need a new doc in the near future."

"You have a doctor."

"Megan's expecting in about seven months. I think she'll leave before that, as soon as they get the infirmary up and running again."

This wasn't the time to talk. "I'll think about it."

"Then I'll think about hunting down the man whose efforts to rehabilitate some losers from a big city might destroy this town." Alec gave Nick his number, then gave a casual salute as he rushed along the pathway, taking bites of his sandwich.

"Wow," Sarah said. "I take it Alec doesn't like Gerard."

Nick gently nudged her toward the huge old wooden mill and the old iron bridge beyond, then followed as she quickstepped away from him past an old oak.

"It would seem he's a little bitter," he said. "Alec's always had the attitude that this is his town."

"Of course he does, since he and his mother own half the businesses."

"He takes pride in Jolly Mill. Always has." He reached her side and kept up the swift pace. "That's not necessarily a bad thing."

"Alec's probably not the only one who feels the way he does about Gerard." She looked up at him, her face flushing slightly from exertion. "Small towns don't take to change quickly, but do you think someone from here would have committed murder on the cliffs to run Gerard off?"

"Only someone crazy, and though some of our citizens are eccentric, I don't know any sociopaths."

"We don't know everyone in town anymore. I'd love to find out who called Edward out of the building just before the explosion."

"At first he thought it was a church member weeping, though he didn't recognize the number."

"Man or woman?"

Nick shortened his steps and took her hand. "He thought it was a woman, but only because those who have called him sobbing are typically of the female persuasion. He couldn't identify the gender. He didn't hear deep, gut-wrenching sobs, just truncated breathing, quick and filled with emotion." Nick led her toward the old grain mill that had been established before the Civil War. "The explosion hit before he could get a word from his caller, and for some time afterward he was stunned."

Sarah stepped up on the wooden walkway that skirted the land side of the mill. She peered through the windows into the deserted building and tried a door. It was locked. "Has anyone looked at the reports Chaz filed?"

"I got a look at them. His words were so precise and to the point as to be shorthand. Gerard spoke with his father, and Judge Collins said his son was unlike himself lately."

"You don't think he was involved—"

"Not actively, but I think his youth made him susceptible to a threat, and obviously the threat was real. Someone probably convinced him his family would be in danger if he reported the truth."

"Yes, but who? Did you ever see him talking to anyone from town?"

"I'm not the one to ask."

"You've been here the past three weeks—you must have seen something." Sarah took Nick's hand briefly as she reached the other side of the walkway and stepped down into the grass. Her hand didn't linger. "All I knew about the explosion was that it was from a gas leak."

"I believe that was a misdirection."

"Our parents weren't killed by a gas leak explosion?"

"I'm not saying they weren't, I'm just saying I doubt Chaz's story. Because of the threat, I don't think Chaz wrote down his real findings. I think someone suspected that Gerard's infirmary nurse saw the act."

"You truly believe that?"

"I'm just working through it logically."

"You think she might have seen someone, or said something to Chaz or even the killer that marked her for death?" Sarah was reading his mind, as she often had all those years ago.

"Pure supposition, but yes, and Gerard agrees it could have been the case."

"So we're talking about collateral damage?"

He hated the expression, because it meant someone took life very lightly, but wasn't that true? That was the nature of murder. "I doubt that poor nurse was the object of our killer's hatred. She was in the wrong place at the wrong time. But unless our killer was simply in a rage against people in the ministry, some of our loved ones might also have been collateral damage."

Nick saw goose bumps rise on Sarah's arms, and she hugged them close to her stomach. She wasn't a member of any police force and wasn't accustomed to the seedier side of life. She was a kindergarten teacher whose most difficult job until three weeks ago was handling a problem child. She didn't need to be involved in finding her parents' killer.

"What a nightmare," she muttered as she picked up speed again.

"Exactly. Now that I think about it, I don't see a lot of people resenting Gerard for his move here. He's pretty much proven himself this past year. He hires locals to teach new skills to those who can no longer find jobs in their fields, so he has less opposition than he might have had, since this area's in a job slump, too. He either helps the families relocate where their skills are needed, or they learn a new trade. I see nothing to oppose, and none of his families have caused trouble."

Sarah walked a few seconds in silence. "Are you sure about that?"

Nick frowned at her.

"Sorry," she said. "Do we know for sure he didn't bring a killer in? How well does he screen the newcomers?"

"That's one question Alec's been asking. All I can say is that Gerard Vance is one of the best judges of character I know, and he's bringing in mostly families in which both parents lost their jobs and couldn't make house payments."

"So you think Gerard's a better judge of character than you are?"

The question stabbed at him. "What does that mean?"

She shrugged. "You always seemed to be able to read people well." She sounded slightly out of breath as they rushed toward the bridge.

"I once thought I had some powers of observation, but I've apparently lost them if I ever had them to begin with."

"Why do you say that?"

"I used to be able to tell if a patient was faking pain for a fix of narcotics. I moonlighted in the E.R. and learned the drill. But when one of my clinic patients decided to sue me for something completely out of my realm of influence, I was flummoxed."

"I'm so sorry. That had to be hard."

"Even though I won the case, I lost faith in people." How many hours had he and Sarah spent down here along the creek, sharing thoughts, dreams, hopes for the future? Maybe returning to this place stimulated the need to talk. "When my marriage fell apart, that did it for me. I don't feel capable of completing this investigation, but no one else was doing it."

"I know you're capable, Nick."

Nick touched Sarah's shoulder. "Alec's suspicious right now, but don't forget he's a war vet. He doesn't trust easily after what he's seen and experienced. His problem with Gerard is the rehab center. Alec's nervous about the homeless Gerard's bringing to town. I think they'll eventually work things out."

Sarah gave him a brief smile. "I'm glad you're investigating. I don't know what I'd do if you weren't here."

"I do. You'd have come and collected Emma and taken her safely home. I'm the one who talked you into staying."

"I don't have that much control over Emma. And speaking of whom…" She cupped her hands beside her mouth and called up the hill. "Emma! Sweetie, are you up there? Emma!" Her voice echoed once, then fell silent.

They listened. No answer.

"She said you never wanted to return here," Nick said.

Sarah walked beside him in silence for a moment. "I was the one who didn't want to leave when my family moved to St. Louis. If we hadn't, things might have been different." Again, she looked up the hill. "Emma?"

"And yet you didn't want to return."

Sarah didn't reply, but her steps slowed.

Nick watched her. Questions arose that had aggravated him since they'd received word of Emma's birth nearly nine months after their move.

"What if someone's attempting to turn the rest of Jolly Mill against Gerard?" Sarah said. "Hit the innocent, let others blame Gerard for placing the innocent in harm's way to begin with, and he gets run out of town."

Nick shortened his steps to match hers. "I think you and I both need to get acquainted with Jolly Mill again. We've been gone too long to know this place intimately anymore."

"Then we'd better do it quickly, or we'll have more friends in harm's way."

Nick glanced at his watch. Dad would be out on the creek by now. He seldom took his cell phone with him fishing, but perhaps today was an exception, with the Russell girls in town. Nick pulled out his phone and hit speed dial. The phone only rang twice before Dad answered.

"Nick, I'm with the Coopers." His voice held

the heavy load of compassion and angst that often affected him when a church member died.

Nick slowed his steps at last. "So you know."

"Yes. The sheriff's here."

"I'm not sure you're safe."

"I'm safe, but I'm not sure about you. Where are you?"

"Chasing Emma. We're near the old bridge. Alec was with Sarah and me until we separated to search. We're about to cross the bridge and go up the hill. Isn't that where you think she'd go?"

Dad groaned. "Why didn't I just cancel my fishing expedition and take her myself? She's a feisty one."

Nick hesitated. "That's what you used to say about Mom."

"Yes, son, I know. She puts me in mind of your mother."

"I asked Alec to find Gerard, but I think I'll have to do the calling, with the bad blood between them."

"Then get him called."

"Yes."

"Keep Sarah calm."

"I know, Dad. Take care of the Coopers. See you in a short time, I hope." As soon as he disconnected, he turned to find Sarah crossing over the bridge ahead of him.

He caught up with her and took her hand. "Dad's worried about you." He tugged gently to slow her down.

She glanced up at him, and he saw moisture in her eyes. "How old was Chaz?"

"Early twenties. Very early. Probably twenty-two. Dad could tell you, I'm sure."

"I can't help thinking he was probably six or seven when I lived here. He was probably one of those little children who rode their bikes up and down the streets when the roads were gravel.... They loved to skid their tires."

"Yeah. I know."

"What kind of monster could have done this to him, Nick?"

"We'll figure that out as we go, but your cousin didn't say anything about a wound of any kind on Chaz?"

"He appeared to have drowned."

"That's a different M.O."

"Oh, please don't tell me you think there's more than one person doing the killing," Sarah said.

"That's not my forte. We need Gerard. I'm not a cop. We're in over our heads."

"You think?" she drawled. "So what's his take on it?"

"Now that they've found Chaz, I don't know."

"My cousin John is in line for a promotion to

detective. Maybe we could use his help, too. He's already offered to take time off and come join us."

"I heard you tell him no."

"He has no authority here."

"Agreed, but keeping close phone contact would be wise, I think." He paused a moment. "We've got some climbing to do." He nodded toward the hillside past the bridge.

"Let's get to it."

As they stepped onto the bridge, he glanced over the side. "Mom told me the school always had a bonfire the first night of football. That's when they had freshman initiation. Some of the guys got pretty mean and threw the freshmen off this bridge into the creek until one guy broke his ankle."

"Shelby was disappointed that they stopped the tradition before we reached ninth grade."

Their footsteps echoed on the old wooden pavement. "Of course she was. She couldn't exist without some kind of excitement taking place around her all the time."

Sarah glanced at him. "True, but in your eyes, Shelby could do no wrong."

Her words surprised him. "You really think that?"

"Who could blame you? Half the class felt the same way."

"I wasn't the proper half of the class."

She shrugged and glanced toward the water. "I

remember exploring this all the way downstream until it emptied into Shoal Creek."

"In that inflatable raft we bought at the garage sale," Nick said. "Shelby wasn't the only one who enjoyed some excitement."

"I didn't enjoy the trouble it got us into." Sarah paused for a moment to catch her breath.

He stopped and turned back to her. "Well, we were only ten. What parent would have allowed a child to float two miles along this creek?"

"I can identify with our parents a lot better now." Sarah glanced up at Nick. "Still, it was fun."

He studied the tense, reflective, well-memorized curves of her face. Fun was only one description he would use to describe their friendship. She'd been his best friend. How drastically life had changed when her family moved away.

"Think you can make it up the hillside?" he teased. "You sound pretty winded already."

She dabbed at the perspiration running down her neck. "You try running after kindergarteners all day and see if you don't develop some stamina."

They scrambled from the bridge and rushed into the grassy, unused road on the other side.

"Maybe Emma's love of excitement comes naturally," Nick said.

"Of course it does."

"You and I both loved a good romp along the creek or exploration of the cave."

She stepped in front of Nick into the deepening grass. It was warm enough for snakes to be out, but she showed no fear. She used to be terrified of the littlest of harmless garter snakes.

"Um, Sarah, I should take point. Dad mentioned seeing copperheads in the area."

That gave her pause, and when she slowed, he moved ahead. It astounded him that even in the midst of their worry about Emma, he was lost in memories of the past with Sarah, and aware of the woman she had become.

"Emma!" Sarah called up the hillside.

Still no answer.

"Alec mentioned how much Emma resembled my mom's picture at school," he said over his shoulder.

Sarah didn't reply. He glanced over his shoulder and saw her staring into the distance, nibbling on her lower lip.

"He compared Mom to Emma."

"Of course he did. He'd already heard about the red VW parked at Edward's house. Anyone would jump to the conclusion that she was family. A cousin, maybe."

Something about the tone in her voice disturbed him. It wasn't quite right, and he hated the suspicion he felt growing.

"Are you going to climb the hill, or are you just plain tuckered out?" she asked.

Nick scrambled off the grassy road and onto one

of the rock paths they once used to climb the hillside. "Remember the weeks just before you and your family moved away?"

"It was the first time I really felt as if I fit into my all-black clothing. I went into mourning."

"Then of course you recall the huge uproar about the party Nora Thompson had in their big old barn just a week before your family moved away."

"You do realize Shelby was the one who talked Nora into throwing that party. Somebody spiked the soda."

Nick grimaced. "Yeah, with ecstasy." He turned and looked back at her, pausing for a moment.

"Running out of breath?" she taunted.

"Don't change the subject. No one remembered much about that night. You weren't there."

"I'd warned Shelby I wouldn't be."

"So you couldn't know how weird it was, but Nora and her friends noticed things were getting strange, good church kids getting giggly and silly even more than normal. Nora, Carmen and Kirstie even searched some of the kids' purses and coats to see if they could find any signs of illegal drugs. Nora told Dad later that there was no smell of alcohol anywhere, so she and the girls gathered up all the food and sodas, cake, snacks, every single crumb, and packed it away. Then they kept watch over the kids the whole night. The boys slept in the barn, the girls in Nora's huge house. The next day, after the kids went home, Nora took everything she and the girls had packed up and drove it to an independent lab in Springfield. That's where the lab techs found ecstasy."

"And you were at that party." Sarah moved as if she would step around him, but he turned and continued up the hill.

"I was there. Shelby was there. Nora, Carmen and Kirstie were good chaperones, but nobody can control a crowd poisoned with ecstasy."

All he heard behind him as he climbed was Sarah's breathing. "Shelby was sick that night," she told him at last.

"No, she wasn't. Shelby was with me sometime that night. I don't remember a lot, but I do remember that much."

Again, nothing but Sarah's labored breathing.

"Sarah, could you just tell me, is Shelby Emma's birth mother?" He kept walking, didn't turn to look down at her.

"I know what you're thinking, but I can promise you Shelby isn't Emma's birth mother, Nick. I should know that better than anybody. I—"

A scream reached them from the top of the hill. It was Emma.

SEVEN

Nick hurtled up the hill barely ahead of Sarah. If she could have flown she'd have winged her way past him to the place where that one brief cry had originated. Instead, she allowed Nick to help her when she stumbled over boulders, and lift her over a huge trunk of a fallen tree.

"Emma!" Nick shouted.

There was no reply.

Terror ripped through Sarah's chest like a thousand serrated knives, and for a moment she thought the day might go black on her. But she kept running, tripping through deep grass, letting Nick take her hand and pull her forward.

Why had Emma insisted on coming here? How awful to imagine her fallen, broken body somewhere above them.

Sarah stumbled against another boulder, and Nick caught her and shoved her upward ahead of him along the rocky path they had once used to make their way to the cave. She remembered this terrain, though much of it had changed. She had no doubt the scream had come from the conference center—she'd been there often enough with Nick.

Why had Alec insisted on taking the shorter way? If they'd taken it instead, they'd have reached that spot by now. But that meant he should be there, shouldn't he? Unless he'd stopped to talk to Gerard.

Either Sarah had stayed in better shape than she'd thought, or her terror for her daughter was giving her superhuman strength. Multiple visions flew through her mind—horrible thoughts of Emma injured, Emma's body mangled. It gave her increased energy and speed until she slid again on a steep part of the trail.

Nick caught her and helped her up the path. "Keep going, we'll get there."

They barely had breath to talk, and Sarah fought the images of Emma in her mind by replaying her answer to Nick's question. How long had he wondered? All this time?

As she scrabbled up toward the top of the hill, she realized the truth must come out about Emma's heritage. It should have long ago. The whole truth. Shelby was not Emma's birth mother, but if Nick was her father he needed to know; it was becoming more and more obvious that he was. First, they had to get to Emma.

Sarah only prayed Alec had also heard the cry and would make his way to them. "Nick, can you get a signal on your phone?"

He pulled it out. "No."

More nightmare images of Emma's broken body continued to urge Sarah upward, and she forced them from her mind.

What a joke it must have been to some wicked soul to watch a bunch of kids who'd tried to remain pure, lose control and allow their hormones to hold sway. Was someone up at the conference center getting the same kind of sick fun making Emma scream? Hurting her?

Sarah gained the top of the cliff. Nick caught up with her, took her hand and together they raced the final distance along the hilltop to the secluded lodge where their parents had spent so many good times together with a strong fellowship of others in their ministerial alliance.

"Emma!" Sarah cried. When they entered a copse of oaks, the sight and scent of charred wood nearly took her to her knees. She imagined the power of the explosion that had taken her parents. It was this very place that they had died. She stumbled onto the steps of the burned-out shell and covered her face. "Oh, no."

Nick caught her and held her up. "What did you see? Did you hear something?" He raised his head. "Emma!"

Sarah shook her head and straightened. "No. They just died here, is all." She scrambled to her feet and rushed onto the slab porch.

The front door of the log lodge stood half open, and it was all that remained upright. Only spikes of logs reached upward, charred furniture, a floor littered with debris that hadn't yet been cleaned up. Of course, it didn't matter that yellow crime-scene tape surrounded the lodge; that wouldn't have stopped Emma from crossing it.

"Emma!" Sarah called.

"Honey, are you here?" Nick shouted.

The rhythmic sound of running steps reached them, and Alec appeared through the wreckage. He came clambering up onto the porch and into the destroyed lodge. "I was looking for Gerard and heard a scream."

"Emma." Sarah started down the hallway that led to the sleeping quarters.

Nick stopped her. "You might fall through."

"What if that happened to Emma?" She pulled free and continued. "Honey? Emma? Are you here? It's Sarah. Please answer me, sweetie. You're scaring us."

"Sarah, look," Alec said, pointing to the floor. "We're tracking fresh mud."

Nick caught Sarah's arm. "There aren't any other tracks but ours."

"She hasn't been here?" Sarah asked.

They spread out and searched the building, stepping carefully over gaping holes in the floor, until Sarah reached the back stoop, where fresh, muddy footprints led down some concrete steps. She recognized the tread of Emma's favorite running shoes. Beside the steps was an opening to a storm cellar. The wooden door had burned with the rest of the house. Something red fluttered in a slight breeze.

"Nick!" She scrambled through the remnants of a screen door and down the steps to the cellar, where Emma lay face down, head down, as if she'd taken a headlong tumble.

"Oh, please God, please let her—"

A soft moan interrupted her panicked prayer as she knelt at Emma's head, where her dark hair tumbled into her face. "Honey? Can you hear me?" She reached out to brush the hair back.

"Don't touch her." Nick's shadow blocked the light as he joined Sarah beside their daughter. "Don't move her, and don't let her move." He knelt two steps below Emma's head.

She moaned again, and this time her voice sounded stronger.

"Emma, we're here." His voice was deep and reassuring. "I need you to hold still if you can hear me. If you can, say yes."

Another soft moan, and then a whispered "Yes."

Sarah lowered her head to keep from passing out. Thank You, God. Thank You, thank You.

"Good," Nick said. "That's good. Be sure not to move until I assess for injuries. Can you tell me what happened?"

"No," she squeaked.

"Did someone hit you?"

"Don't know. How long was I out?"

"Not long, honey," Sarah said.

Alec hovered above them. "I'll call for an ambulance."

Nick stood up. "Let me check her out first. If we can move her, we'll get her to the hospital more quickly than an ambulance could, but call the hospital in Monett and let them know we're bringing a patient in for a CT, maybe more. While you're at it, get a car up here. Use Gerard's. It'll take less time if we can move her ourselves and cell reception is spotty up here."

Alec nodded and left.

Emma groaned and tried to raise her head.

"No!" Nick grabbed her and eased her gently back into the same position. "You can't move yet. I have to make sure you won't injure yourself with movement."

"Hurry. These steps are digging in."

"I know. I'm sorry. Would you wiggle your toes for me? Not your legs, just your toes."

Sarah held her breath and waited while her daughter moved her feet, wiggled her fingers, and even giggled a little when Nick squeezed each leg and arm, testing for any painful areas. He moved quickly, with assurance. He knew what he was doing, and as he continued his exam, Sarah felt herself falling in love with him all over again. This was the man she'd known he'd become one day.

This was Emma's father. A pit viper of guilt shot its poison through her. She pushed it away. Time for that—for reminding herself what happiness she and her parents withheld from Edward and Aunt Peg and Nick for sixteen years—when she knew for sure Emma would be okay.

"Do you feel sick to your stomach?" Nick asked Emma.

"No. Can I get up now?" Her voice was growing stronger every moment.

"Soon, honey." He asked the usual questions to test for mental alertness, and she answered her full name, birthday, year, what day it was.

"I got mad at Sarah and left and I'm sorry, and I went to talk to Carmen, and then got hungry and went to get a smoothie and—ouch!"

Nick's hands stilled at the back of her head where he had been searching for wounds, then he looked at Sarah and nodded to a spot of blood in Emma's hair. "Honey, do you remember how you fell?"

"I…uh…no." She moved both arms and kicked her legs. "But I'm moving, see? The only thing that hurts is my head and the places where these stupid steps are slashing into my skin like shark teeth."

"Do you remember hitting your head on something? Maybe you fell backward and hit your head on the step, then somehow rolled forward?" He gently moved each leg, then each arm, palpated her neck and looked up at Sarah.

"I guess so. I don't remember. Please, can I get up now?"

He nodded to Sarah and together they rolled Emma over and right side up until she was able to sit on a step.

"Are you dizzy?" Nick asked.

Emma grimaced at Sarah. "If I say yes, Sarah will feel sorry for me and then she won't yell at me."

Sarah took that stab without a word.

"Emma Russell, this is not something to joke about." Nick's voice was suddenly firm and filled with authority—the kind of authority Sarah wished she had with her daughter. "Are you dizzy?"

"A little, yeah."

"What do you last remember before you woke up?" he asked.

She scrunched her lips together. "That cashier at the diner told me where this place was, then she said I shouldn't come up here because there was still crime-scene tape around it. But nobody's doing anything about the crime, so I figured why shouldn't I, right?"

"Wrong," Nick said. "What else? Which way did you come up here?"

"I took the new bridge and passed the rehab center. Wow. Cool place. I didn't think it'd be so big. I saw the place that exploded."

"Then what?" Nick asked.

Emma looked up at him, her eyes so like her father's that Sarah found herself holding her breath. "Well, first I walked around this place and kind of... you know...cried a little. Because, you know, this is where they died."

"I feel the same way, honey," Sarah said.

Emma nodded, then winced and reached up toward the back of her head. Nick grabbed her hand and lowered it.

"Anyway, I saw fresh footprints in the mud at the side of the building, and I thought, hey, if someone was here, maybe they could tell me something. So I started calling out." She frowned. "I think. After that, I don't remember. I don't know how I fell or hit my head."

An SUV with the logo Vance Renewal on the door pulled up to the entrance and a giant, blond, broad-shouldered man stepped out wearing well-worn jeans, boots and a camo T-shirt.

"I got a cryptic message from our favorite city father that you were in need of my services." The man, obviously Gerard Vance, the ex-cop, had a deep voice with a definite Texas drawl. "He was running and talking on his cell at the same time." His attention went to Sarah and Emma.

Nick stepped forward and shook his hand. "Glad you came, Gerard. We're in some trouble. Can you give us a ride to the hospital?"

"Sure thing." Gerard released Nick's hand, patted him on the shoulder and walked toward Emma and Sarah as Nick explained the situation. Together, the two men gently eased Emma to her feet, waited for her response, then when she remained steady, they helped her into the front passenger seat of the car.

Nick opened the backseat door for Sarah, closed it, got in the other side, and Gerard eased smoothly down the road on the way to the hospital.

Sarah was so glad she hadn't eaten anything since early morning because she knew she'd have lost it in the ex-cop's nice, clean SUV.

To Nick's relief, the E.R. waiting room wasn't filled to capacity, and a tech took Emma straight back via wheelchair, with Emma protesting all the way that she could walk, she wasn't an invalid and she was sure the techs had more important things to do than coddle her. Then she started apologizing for all the trouble she caused. When the tears began, Sarah was there, talking softly. But she was obviously alarmed by her sister's behavior.

Nick waited until Gerard returned from parking his SUV. "Hey, if you want to take off, Dad told me he's on his way here. I know you're busy today."

"You kidding? You realize, don't you, that half of Jolly Mill will be here after word spreads through town like wildfire? I've been around long enough to have learned that much. This could be a break in our case."

"Did you know Chaz was found drowned this morning in Spring River?"

Gerard's expression darkened. "Tragic. Believe it or not, Alec relented enough to tell me that much before running downhill, probably toward his car. I think we've got him on board completely now. We should expect to see him pulling up outside any time, along with several others. Most folks still think of the Russells as part of the town."

"They'll fill the room." Nick couldn't stop a smile, despite the tense situation. His old, close-knit hometown was appealing to him more all the time. Except, of course, for the killer that might reside there.

"The outpatient waiting room will be empty today, this being Saturday." Gerard's deep voice and Texas twang drew the attention of some of the people in the waiting room and even an admiring glance from the secretary behind the glass partition.

"Want to direct traffic there?" Nick asked.

"I'll take care of that. I'm sure the E.R. staff will appreciate it. I've been here a few times, so the staff knows me. I'll call the clinic and let Carmen know so she won't be blindsided. I need to talk to Megan, anyway."

"I'd appreciate it." Nick glanced toward the doors through which Emma and Sarah had passed.

"I know you want to join them," Gerard said.

"More than anything. She doesn't need to face this alone, but do you really think a killer would have the guts to come through those doors with half the population of Jolly Mill hovering nearby?"

"If you lived in a tiny town and you'd just made an attempt at your sixth murder, would you raise suspicions by making yourself scarce, or would you blend in with the crowd to allay those suspicions?" Gerard asked.

"I bow to your experience. You believe someone from our town attacked Emma."

"I can't rule it out anymore."

"But do you think someone might have followed Emma up the hill? If so, wouldn't Alec have seen?"

Gerard sighed. "Unfortunately, it could have been any number of scenarios. In my years on the force, I saw pretty much everything, so I tend to suspect wrongdoing until it's ruled out. I've been doing follow-up background checks on my rehab families, covering all the bases."

"Find anything?"

"Nope. And if I had any questions I wouldn't cover for them. We'll have to keep looking."

"We need more eyes on the town, but we need to know which eyes we can trust," Nick said. "Emma might eventually recall more, but she has retrograde amnesia."

"You should go in there for Sarah's sake, Nick.

Sit with her. She doesn't look like she's holding together too well right now."

"When Dad gets here, send him back, would you? Sarah's always had a special connection to my parents, and Dad has a way of comforting those most in need of it."

"Meanwhile, I think I'll fire up some of the old radar from my Corpus Christi street days and see if I can do some detecting. I'll start mingling if our citizens come in."

Sarah stood in the doorway to the E.R. exam room, fists clenched as she watched Emma being wheeled away from her. Despite the radiation, she wanted to be there when they put her into the machine, wanted to hold her hand and tell her everything would be okay, but the tech refused the company.

Before Sarah had a chance to melt into a puddle of anxiety on the E.R. floor, Nick stepped around a corner past the central desk and walked toward her. She rushed to him, throwing her arms around his nicely firm abs as she buried her face in his chest. The comfort of his return hug brought more relief than any antianxiety med could have done.

"She's going to be okay, Sarah." His strong voice rumbled in his chest and she closed her eyes as it echoed through her mind. She hadn't felt safe or protected since the explosion killed her parents. Their parents.

She released her death grip on him. "I don't know how much more I can take, and please don't tell anyone I said that, because I'll do whatever I have to for Emma."

He kept an arm around her and guided her back into the empty exam room, then pulled the visitor chair over for her to sit down. "The CT shouldn't take long. The E.R. doesn't look too busy, so I doubt she'll have much of a wait. The reading will be the only thing the doc will have to wait on, and I learned from the nurse that there's a radiologist on call who has a pretty quick turnaround." He pulled the rolling doctor stool over and sank onto it so he could face her. He took her hands. "At the risk of repeating myself, you're not alone."

She allowed those words to settle over her. "I'm beginning to believe you." And she never got tired of hearing him say those words.

"Dad's on his way here, along with half the town, I'm afraid."

"It's their way."

"Maybe it's the doctor in me, but I never understood the tendency for a huge group of people to crowd the hospital to attend to one friend."

She grinned at him. "Oh, come on, Nick. Before you were a doctor, you were a preacher's kid. We

PKs know people feel a need to be close so they can pray better."

"Illogical. God can hear prayer wherever it's coming from."

"You're too much like me. I like my interpersonal exchanges to be in small groups, not huge clumps of people all talking at once."

"This time we could be catching a break." Nick glanced over his shoulder, then shoved the door shut. "If Emma's head injury wasn't an accident, Gerard thinks the culprit might show up with others from Jolly Mill."

Sarah was unable to suppress a shudder. "I hate this."

"Gerard can read people. If he sees anything out of place, he'll check it out. Come to think of it, Dad's a pretty good judge of character, too. I might have him mingle."

"Edward likes to think the best of people, and he'll be uncomfortable watching members of his own congregation. You won't. Why don't you do the mingling?"

"Okay, then when Dad gets here, Gerard will send him back so you won't have to be all alone in this room. I'll join the others and get to work."

Sarah wrapped her cold, bare arms over her chest and rubbed them. "Edward can wait with Emma. I'll join you when he gets here."

"You need to focus on Emma."

"I didn't have time to explain to the doctor that she doesn't typically chatter like a squirrel—"

"It is Emma we're talking about. It's a family trait."

"But she never trips over her own words, and something was frightening her. Maybe she'd just picked up on your suspicions, but when they were wheeling her through the E.R., her gaze darted all over the room, from person to person, paranoid."

"After what she's been through, that's not unusual. We'll have to watch the abnormal behavior. How would you feel if the doctor decides to keep her in the hospital for observation?"

Sarah shook her head. "Only if I can bring a weapon in with me, and that's not allowed in a hospital. You're a doctor, Megan's not far away, we don't need the hospital for anything. Not enough security here."

"What if Gerard and I took turns guarding her room tonight?"

Sarah met Nick's gaze. "Someone was able to sneak past Gerard and destroy his infirmary with his nurse inside."

"Even more reason for us to take precautions. Chaz is dead and Emma's injured. I think we don't know enough about what we're dealing with yet. Our culprit has the upper hand and is reigning with extreme prejudice."

"A reign of terror," Sarah said. "Who's next?"

EIGHT

It had always been a family joke that Nick, though an introvert of the first order, had chosen a profession in which he worked with people constantly, invaded their privacy, personal space, their home lives, worked with staff and sometimes was forced to manage the very crowds of well-wishers he'd complained about to Sarah. He'd had no doubt about his calling from the time he entered high school. God definitely had a sense of humor.

He still didn't like crowds, but he had to admit to himself that Gerard was right as he mingled through the press of people in the outpatient waiting room at Cox Monett Hospital. This was an excellent way to study a lot of people at once without being obvious about it.

There were several members here from Dad's church, old classmates of Nick's, including Alec, who had, as expected, brought his new lady love, Petra Journigan—that was where he'd likely been headed, and who he'd been calling, when he raced past the rehab center, delivering his news to Gerard at a run.

Though Nick and Sarah had been reluctant to leave Emma's exam room, Dad was there now giving her the comfort she desperately needed. Nick had convinced Sarah to help him study the crowd as it grew. No one could console a fretting spirit as naturally as Edward Tyler.

The hallway door opened and Carmen rushed through, blond curls flying everywhere, her typically pretty, open face tight with tension. When she caught sight of Nick and Sarah she rushed to them.

"I ran out of the clinic as soon as I heard. I had to be here. Poor Lynley and Megan are handling it all without me. Anything?"

"No results from the CT yet," Sarah said. "It shouldn't be much longer, and the doctor knows to reach me here."

Carmen clawed at her arms, lips pressed together, eyes squeezed shut for a few seconds before opening them again. "My fault, guys. This was my fault. What was I thinking? I knew about Emma's rambunctious personality, but—"

"You couldn't know everything," Nick said. "Stop blaming yourself."

"If that girl has sustained permanent damage from this, I'll never forgive myself. I promised you I'd send her straight home when she left the clinic this morning, but I thought she was going back to you for breakfast."

"And she should have." Nick couldn't say more with others listening. He scanned the faces of several longtime residents of Jolly Mill. Nora Thompson, Alec's mother, stood talking quietly to one of her and Carmen's oldest friends, Kirstie Marshal, their voices so soft as to be silent. When they spotted Carmen, Nick and Sarah, Nora grabbed Kirstie's arm and they wove their way among the others to her side.

Nora and Kirstie huddled around Sarah, hugging her, commiserating with her, giving her the comfort she obviously needed.

Nora looked up and pulled Nick aside. "Alec told me about your blog. I'm surprised it's taken me this long to find out about it." A tall, exotic woman with midnight black hair, she didn't have to stretch too far to press her lips near his ear. "I know that grim look on Gerard's face, and Alec's more worried than I've seen him in…well, in weeks." She gestured toward her son, who stood with his arm around red-headed, freckled Petra. Typically upbeat and smiling, even Petra looked shaken. It seemed everyone in the room now believed Nick's suspicions, and that made it all the more real. Even Nick's estranged cousin Billy stood in a corner shooting a glare in Petra's direction from time to time. Or was he glaring at Alec?

Hmm. Billy had a crush on Petra in high school, but that was a lifetime ago.

"I'd hoped the sheriff's department would reopen the case and connect the dots," Nick said. "I even sent links to my blog posts."

"I've called the sheriff, too," Nora said. "I have to say I'm disappointed, but they're low on manpower and I have a feeling something's up, probably another meth lab bust, where they need all hands on deck. I'm so afraid we're on our own."

"We're never on our own."

Nora grimaced. "Of course I know God's watching over us, but don't you think it'd be wise for us to protect ourselves, as well?"

"God has sent us some good people. We have Gerard, Alec, Dad, who does know how to handle a weapon, and will, to protect his own, even if he is a preacher. We aren't helpless in Jolly Mill, and now that everyone is aware there is danger, all will be on the lookout."

Nora's dark eyes narrowed as she looked up at him. "Unfortunately, there's a wild card, my dear. We don't know who's doing all this. Everyone is afraid Emma was attacked, but by whom?" She glanced around the room as if she, too, suspected the killer might be here.

"Another question is why," Nick said. He studied Nora for a moment. Though a pillar of their tiny society, Nora Thompson had a...somewhat textured history. Last year she had risked her life, her freedom and her good name in town to protect her son's future—which hadn't needed protecting—and to keep Gerard Vance from moving his rehab center.

And then, according to Dad, when Gerard won the zoning vote from the town council to establish his project, not only had Nora befriended him with every bit of her genteel hospitality from that time on, she had volunteered her own services. She now taught night classes in business administration at the center.

Sometimes Nick wondered why the abrupt change of heart.

Nora took a few steps away from the gathered group and strolled toward the outpatient entrance. She glanced over her shoulder and gestured with her eyes for Nick to join her. "Carmen told me Emma couldn't remember how she hit her head." Nearing her mid-fifties, Nora wore three-inch heels like a runway model.

He caught up with her. "Retrograde amnesia. She remembers nothing about the fall."

"So she could have tripped."

"Absolutely." Nick didn't believe that for a minute. "The injury on her head might match the edge of a stair step." Trying not to be obvious, he considered Nora for a moment. She wasn't above using political misdirection and community trust to leverage her businesses, but how far would she go?

"Never play poker." Her sultry voice wrapped around him.

"I'm sorry?"

"I can see what you're thinking by the way you're not looking at me. I might be a killer, but I'm not a murderer."

He met her gaze. Nora had killed two men in her life, though according to Dad both killings had been justified in court as self-defense. The first man was Nora's abusive husband when Nick and Alec were still in high school. The second was Kirstie Marshal's estranged husband last year, after Nora suspected him of poisoning Kirstie for the fortune of a dying uncle. Both men discovered Nora wasn't to be trifled with.

"No, Nora, you're not a murderer."

She turned in an elegant pirouette and perused the community of folks who had gathered. "Most of these people are either members of your father's church, or they once belonged to Mark Russell's congregation. They're here to show support. Good people, all of them. Or rather, maybe all but one."

Her words didn't surprise him. Nora was insightful, cunning, tough. She was also loyal to those she knew and loved. She was loyal, for instance, to the citizens of Jolly Mill, but if she suspected anyone but her son to be the killer, Nick wondered if she might take the role of executioner into her own hands in defense of other innocents. She'd do as fine a job of sheriffing as she did everything else—with consummate skill and a deadly aim.

"You have a suspect in mind?" Despite her poor choice of husbands—that was a long time ago—he valued her opinion.

She raised a well-arched brow. "Still thinking. I can't imagine why anyone would kill people in the ministry, but I've always been a small-town girl with typical Bible belt values, so killing a servant of God is like attacking God Himself. Still, I'm as human as the next person, and you do realize your cousin Billy and his father were at outs over the restaurant?"

"Why would that put ministers in danger?"

"Your mother was a fabulous cook, and she worked with your uncle Will when he ran the place."

"She didn't want to own it, though."

"I could easily see your mother running that place. She and I even talked about selling my specialty cookies from the counter with coffee."

"But Mom—"

"I'm just bouncing some ideas off you. Your suspicions about your father being a target over the Spring River toxic spill might also have some merit, but we don't have anything to back up either of our theories. And poor Cindy Rouse, the nurse at the rehab center? I don't understand her death at all. There was so little connection between her death and the others."

"Sarah and I considered she and Chaz might

have been collateral damage. Maybe they knew too much."

Nora's eyes narrowed as she thought about that. She nodded. "Then you'll agree that there was probably only one target. All but one death might have been collateral damage. Has your father mentioned any connection Cindy might have had to the retreat that weekend?"

"She attended Dad's church, so she took snacks and lemonade to the conference center a couple of times for their breaks."

"Did she, now? Do you suppose she might have seen something while she was there that could make her suspicious after the explosion?"

"Such as?"

"No idea," Nora said. "I can't believe she would be targeted for her work in the infirmary."

"Did she and Chaz know one another?"

"Most likely. Both were young, single, attractive."

"It would stand to reason that if she did see something suspicious, she might have said something to Chaz about it, since she knew he was investigating the explosion."

Nora tapped Nick's arm. "Yes. He was very anxious about the whole thing. I remember talking to him once, and when I mentioned the investigation, his eyes bugged out, he started to sweat and he excused himself almost immediately."

"Until the second explosion, no one even suspected there might be a murderer in our midst. Did you notice anyone else around you at the time you spoke with Chaz? Someone who might have overheard?"

Nora paused, and Nick couldn't miss the trepidation in her eyes. "We were in the clinic," she said. "Poor kid was so stressed he needed something to calm him down." Her eyes widened. "I just violated HIPAA."

"I won't tell."

"No other patients were around. Megan and Carmen were finishing up for the night, so they were the only two who observed his behavior. No, wait, Alec had come to collect a deposit to drop by the bank. All of them are trustworthy, Nick, you know that. Chaz was simply terrified, as we know now, and at the time we didn't know what was wrong. He wasn't talking."

"Did you know him well enough to suspect he might have been involved in any way? Sarah suggested he might have taken drastic measures to draw some attention to his powers of observation in his new job title."

Nora hesitated. "I never would have thought it, but here's a scenario for you. He didn't know the conference center was in use that weekend. He caused a leak in the gas line so it would blow over the weekend, and Cindy saw him and mentioned something to him, forcing him to do the same to her to save himself. But Chaz was raised by a good family, and the guilt became too much for him. He could have covered himself, then in a fit of angst, rammed the balustrade at the bridge to escape the overwhelming guilt."

"Has Alec discussed this with you?"

"As if he would. He thinks I'm breakable." She tapped Nick's arm with perfectly manicured nails. "My scenario doesn't explain Emma's fall today, unless it was an accident."

"Or Emma was followed because she was the youngest Russell daughter?"

Nora's dark eyes widened. "Sweetheart, I can't imagine anyone in our town being filled with so much hatred they'd resort to killing an innocent child."

"I've reluctantly considered the possibility of escorting Sarah and Emma back to Sikeston."

"If Chaz wasn't the culprit, then our killer can drive there just as easily. Besides, I doubt they have a place to stay in Sikeston that has alarms set up on every door, plus a killer Doberman on the prowl. Carmen's also got a good eye with a weapon in her hand."

"Unfortunately, half the town probably expects them to stay there."

"I see that as a good thing." Nora began her graceful stroll back to join Kirstie and Carmen.

Nick watched the group with increasing frustration. He knew every person in the room, and though he'd learned to read faces and body language well, he'd seen nothing that alerted him.

Billy Parker walked across the room toward Alec and Petra, and it wasn't difficult to read the jealousy in his expression. That didn't surprise Nick. He could imagine how quickly Billy had jumped at the chance to hire Petra when she'd returned to town. He'd always had a special fondness for her.

When Billy reached the couple, Alec stiffened for a moment, but Petra whispered something in his ear. He glared at Billy and walked away.

A few seconds later, Petra laid a hand on Alec's arm and smiled up at him. He practically jerked from her touch. She looked hurt and stepped away, crossing her arms and hunching her shoulders. Alec shook his head and put a hand on her back, whispered in her ear. She leaned against him again.

He looked like a man in love.

Gerard strolled to Nick's side. "Some kind of triangle going on with them?" He nodded toward the two lovebirds. "Your cousin doesn't approve?"

"Old grudges, I think. I'm sure Alec's as distracted as the rest of us are. You and he still not on speaking terms?"

"We're on nodding terms. I believe my wife will help him decide in my favor. He shouldn't complain—Megan's quadrupled the patient load since she arrived."

"He's unhappy about something," Nick said.

"You're telling me. You don't suspect Alec could be—"

Nick raised his hand. "He might be a tough business negotiator, but we both know he's not going to resort to violence to get the rehab center out of town. It's possible your nurse's death could have happened because she witnessed something she shouldn't have."

"Cindy?"

"Do you know if she and Chaz were seeing each other socially?"

"She never mentioned it to me."

"Though my cousin had the retreat catered, Cindy took snacks to the conference center both days. She belonged to Dad's church."

Gerard closed his eyes and shook his head. "Not much to go on, though. Lots of 'might have beens.' Megan told me something a few months ago, and I'd forgotten about it until recently. It's possible Alec blamed his father's death on Mark Russell. Nora might be concerned about that."

Nick glanced toward Nora, who was talking quietly with her friends and Sarah near the door. Everyone in town had discovered last year that Nora had killed her abusive husband in self-defense many years ago when he went after her once too often. "She was careful to keep the abuse a secret. Why would he blame Mark?"

"He was about thirteen, I think, when he confided in Mark that he thought his dad was hurting his mom. Mark tried to talk to Eaton and it only made things worse, apparently. Amazing the silent abuse that takes place in a quiet, safe-seeming town. When everything finally came out last year, Nora had to hire a team of attorneys to keep her out of jail. It was a shock to the whole town, and though Nora kept her cool through the whole thing, Alec nearly lost it. He developed a full-blown case of PTSD that he'd managed to control since his stint in Afghanistan."

"What about the sheriff?" Nick asked. "Who calls a pastor to intervene in a violent family disturbance?"

"A young kid who looked up to Mark as a role model for a father. He believed Mark failed him. He did end up calling the sheriff eventually, and of course, Nora covered it up to protect the Thompson name."

Nick and Gerard were still watching the crowd when the doors swung open and a tech pushed Emma through in a wheelchair. A wide bandage of gauze circled her head like a crown. The crowd surged toward her, surrounding her, gently hugging her and Sarah. The chatter doubled in the room.

Emma was going to be okay. The room grew noisy for a few moments as the community of Jolly Mill showered the Russell girls with their love and promises of protection. Emma's expression told Nick that she was soaking up all the love in the room. Sarah's eyes glistened with unshed tears after Dad announced that Emma was released from the hospital.

Nick met Gerard's gaze and then both of them quickly studied the expressions of members of the crowd. Nick saw nothing out of place except for Alec's hard-eyed glower—and he was also studying the crowd, on guard.

The man caught Nick's gaze and wandered over to him, arms crossed over his chest. "I don't like this. We need to get that little gal far away from here. Jolly Mill isn't safe."

Petra stepped up beside Alec and placed a hand on his arm. "Honey, Jolly Mill's probably the safest place for her right now." She had a soft, gentle voice. She gestured to the people surrounding the Russell girls. "She's safer with all the folks in our town watching out for her."

"How can she be watched around the clock?"

"You're a soldier. You know how," she said.

Alec paused a moment, staring into Petra's open gaze. He nodded and wandered away.

For once, Petra didn't follow him like his trained pet. She stood beside Nick watching the others. "I remember Sarah from school."

"She was a lot different then."

Petra giggled. "Goth girl. I always thought she

was so cool. I mean, I didn't have the guts, but she did. I wanted to be her."

"Her twin, Shelby? You'd remember her."

Petra rolled her green eyes. "Miss precious cheer-leader, most popular, everybody loved her? Except me. I remember you and Sarah were the item in school."

"Item?" Nick smiled. He watched Sarah, who hovered close to Emma. Her behavior toward her baby sister since she'd arrived this morning had been more maternal than sisterly. How difficult it must be to take on the responsibilities of raising a teenager, especially one with so much energy and curiosity.

"Nick?" Petra said. "You and Sarah?"

"We were good friends. We got into a lot of mischief together."

"That's why nobody else could ever get close to you. I don't think you ever had eyes for anyone but Sarah." Petra leaned closer. "Half the girls in our class were in love with you, and I don't think you ever noticed. You were always watching Sarah."

He laughed out loud at that.

"I had plenty of competition."

Nick blinked at her. "Uh, sorry—"

"Oh, don't worry. Alec's my guy now, but your dad watched out for me when my family moved to town, and I see a lot of him in you." She smiled up into his eyes, and he felt an itch of discomfort.

* * *

Emma tugged on Sarah's arm. "Sis."

"Yes? You okay?"

Emma's eyes narrowed at something across the room. "Her name's Petra, right?"

Sarah looked up to see Nick and Petra talking together and nodded. "I knew her in school. Smart, but no one would've known it from her grades."

"I think she's standing a little too close to Nick," Emma muttered. "I thought she was dating Alec. Maybe she's not as smart as you think if she can't tell the guys apart."

Sarah chuckled. "Old school friends, honey. Relax and focus on getting well."

"The least you could do is make a friendly gesture. You know, like, walk over and slide in between them. With your fist, if you have to."

Sarah's chuckle turned into a giggle, she was so relieved Emma was back to her old self and already playing matchmaker again.

"Well, unlike you, I can tell when a woman's trying to make a move on a man."

Sarah eyed the slightly plump woman with bright red, shoulder-length hair, freckles covering her skin, eyes green and lively. "Nick was nice to her in high school when she was new and lonely. He had a lot of compassion."

"Is that why he spent so much time with you? Because you were lonely and he felt sorry for you?"

"No, I was good in English, and I helped him with his penmanship. Besides, I chose to be alone—he just didn't let me."

"And so you pretended to be Goth so no one would confuse you with your twin? Really, Sarah. You don't know how much that hurt Shelby's feelings?"

Sarah continued to watch Nick and Petra, their shoulders nearly touching. She returned her attention to Emma. "Sorry, honey, but Shelby and I were always like that. We learned to live with it."

Gerard Vance, at least two inches taller than any other person in the room, waved his arms over his head. "Folks, our patient's been released. No reason for us to hang around here. Why don't we all head home?"

Edward stepped forward to push the wheelchair, but Gerard laid a hand on his shoulder. "Pull back for a minute," he said softly. "Others can lead the way." He winked at Emma. "Keep your eyes open."

Sarah held her breath as she watched Emma. There was no sign of recognition as she studied the crowd. She smiled at everyone, thanked them for coming, returned loving hugs from Carmen, Kirstie and Nora, and behaved as if she was at a party until the final visitor left.

"See anything familiar, honey?" Edward asked.

Emma darted a glance up at Sarah. She sniffed and studied the empty room. "I did catch a whiff

of something when I got to the conference center."
She sniffed again. "I smelled it again a few seconds ago."

Sarah reached for Edward's arm. The killer was here?

NINE

Nick's arm came around Sarah before she even had time to panic. "It's okay. We'll check it out." He knelt beside Emma. "What smell caught your attention?"

Emma touched her nose, then scratched it as if it itched. "Fruity? Spicy?"

"Like perfume?" Sarah asked.

Emma grimaced. "It smelled good, but not perfumy, you know?"

"So not a cologne." Gerard nodded to Nick, then took off along the hospital hallway to catch up with the crowd.

Emma looked up at Nick, and he could read the fear in her eyes.

"Don't worry, Emma. Gerard's got a nose like a bloodhound and a voice like a bullhorn, so if someone who smells like fruit and spice was in the room and Gerard finds this person, he'll do some extreme questioning and maybe an in-depth sniff test."

Emma's giggle made Sarah's heart contract with tenderness and love.

"Did anybody come here from the diner?" Sarah asked. "It smelled wonderful there, like cinnamon and bacon and smoked ham." She was suddenly hungry just thinking about it, despite the overwhelming anxiety of the morning. Maybe she was unwinding from the anxiety, knowing how many friends surrounded her, and how many she knew for sure she could trust. "It followed us all the way up the hill, remember, Nick?"

"Emma, did you smell bacon just now? Or ham?"

Emma nodded. "But something more. Not like food."

"Someone else might have brought one of those huge cinnamon rolls from Parker's," Nick said. "Billy was here."

"Nora told us she'd been baking a new spice cookie," Sarah said. "And she smelled wonderful." It had been comforting to spend a few moments with Nora, Kirstie and Carmen, three of Mom's best friends when they lived here, but now that they'd walked out, she lingered beside Edward, basking in the comfort of his presence.

He took her into his big, strong arms and hugged her, and she felt as if some of his strength melted into her, infusing her with courage she knew she wouldn't have without him here. How she loved this man. How she'd missed him.

What would his reaction be when he discovered

Emma was the granddaughter he'd never known—and Aunt Peg would never know?

The truth would have to come out, and soon.

Edward patted her hand and then reached for the wheelchair. "Let's get Emma settled in Gerard's monster SUV. It's going to be okay, sweethearts. I'm not leaving you, and neither will Nick. I've already decided to stay at Carmen's with you tonight." He stepped out into the broad hallway and turned the silent wheelchair to the left. "I'm here so much, the staff trusts me with the wheelchair, especially when they're busy. Emma, you're going to love Carmen's big old teddy bear of a Doberman. Nina might eat an intruder, but she's going to fall in love with you. In fact, I'd be surprised if she didn't stay by your side from the moment the two of you are introduced."

"Really?" Emma looked up at Sarah. She'd wanted her own dog ever since their family dachshund died of old age.

"A lot of animals can sense when someone's sick or in pain. I think you might be able to convince Carmen to let Nina sleep with you tonight, if you don't mind a little snoring," Edward said.

Sarah's steps slowed. "Edward, I need to call our cousin John. If he hears about this from any source besides me, he'll never forgive me."

"Good thought, honey. I'll get Emma safely settled." He raised a hand and waved without stopping the forward motion of the wheelchair.

Sarah pulled her cell phone from her purse and pressed speed dial for John Fred. He answered almost before the first ring ended.

"Hey, cuz, I've tried calling five times."

"Sorry, I've been in the hospital, had my cell off."

"Hospital?"

"She's fine. Bump on the head. Little amnesia."

Silence.

She looked at the screen. She hadn't lost connection. "John?"

"You couldn't have called?" Her cousin seldom raised his voice, but she glanced around the hallway to see if anyone heard his shout. "You couldn't have asked someone else to call?"

"I'm calling now, earliest I could do it, okay? I wanted to wait until I knew she was okay so you wouldn't—"

"Don't you *ever* do that again."

"John, she fell at the conference center where Mom and Dad and Aunt Peg were killed. Nick and I found her on the outside steps that led into the cellar." Sarah took a deep breath. "She had a bump and blood on the back of her head, but she was lying with her head down, face down on the steps. In other words, not a natural position she could have gotten herself into, if you ask me."

"What happened?"

"She's still trying to remember. It seems half the town came to the hospital, and Gerard and Nick are conferring to decide if we might have had a culprit in the waiting area."

"I'm coming to Jolly Mill. I've already spoken to the chief, and—"

"I'm not having this argument with you again, so come on over if you want. I do want you to get something for me, though."

"What?"

"Go back to both houses, mine and my parents', and get out those old albums and scrapbooks Mom and I made of Emma."

A brief silence, and then, "You're going to tell him."

"I'm going to tell them all, most likely the whole town."

"What, you're just going to call them all together and make an announcement? I've got to see this. You know I do." The excitement in his voice nearly quivered through the line. "Don't say anything until I get there."

"No promises."

"Gotta go, cuz. Gotta pack. There's no way I'm letting you face this on your own. I'll be there with scrapbooks as soon as I can, but don't go to bed tonight until I get there."

Nick shook his head, entranced, when the sliding glass doors of the hospital slid back and his father wheeled Emma outside. Half the folks who had come to check on her were already gone, but those still in the parking lot turned and cheered. Emma smiled like a bright-eyed little beauty queen who couldn't believe her good fortune, her dark eyes shining, her long, dark brown hair drifting across her face with the breeze. No wonder Sarah had been so frantic about her baby sister's safety. The child had a tendency to wrap that wide open smile around a person's heart and lock on. Even her typical teenage rebellion was atypical, because of her obviously tender heart.

But something was missing from this picture. Sarah. Nick frowned and gazed around the parking lot. He saw Gerard jumping into his SUV to drive around and pick up their patient, but Sarah had not joined them.

Bloodhound mission forgotten, he rushed to his father's side.

"She's making a call," Dad said before Nick could ask.

John. Of course. "She's still inside?"

Dad nodded. "Don't rush her."

Nick leaned over Emma. "Honey, do you have a headache?"

"Yeah, but don't tell Sarah." Emma rolled her eyes. "It's like, all of a sudden, since the funeral, she's been ten times more hoveracious than Mom ever was."

Nick grinned. "Hoveracious?"

"Tell me you don't know exactly what I mean."

He looked up as Sarah stepped through the doors. His smile died when he saw a sparkle of tears on her face. "Yeah, Emma, I think I know what you mean," he said as Sarah leaned her forehead against Dad's shoulder. Dad immediately released the wheelchair with one hand and wrapped an arm around her.

"She kind of likes you, doesn't she?" Nick said to Emma.

Gerard pulled the SUV up to the wheelchair beneath the awning and jumped out to help get Emma settled.

"Yeah, boy, you could say that." Emma shook her head and did another eye roll.

"Nice, huh?"

Emma shrugged. "If it was healthy, sure." She stood up and glanced over her shoulder at her sister. "She worries too much. It's not good for her."

Sarah acknowledged Emma's statement with a sniff and a watery smile. Nick wanted to take them both in his arms and draw them close. Instead, he turned and helped Gerard get Emma settled while Dad took the wheelchair back into the hospital.

"Front seat again, little lady," Gerard told Emma. "After a knock on the head, you'll be less likely to get carsick if you sit in front."

"I never get carsick."

"Ever had your head whacked before?" Nick asked. "Get in the front. Doctor's orders. It'll protect

Gerard's interior and give me a chance to sit in the back with Sarah."

That wide smile returned. "Oh, really?" Emma glanced toward her sister, then back at Nick, and she winked. "Any ulterior motives?"

Nick opened the back door for Sarah, but she hesitated, her gray-green eyes pensive. "Much as I'd love to ride with you and be teased by Emma for thirty minutes, I don't like the idea of Edward driving home alone." She looped her purse over her shoulder and stepped away from the SUV. "I think he could use some company."

"Hey, Sarah," Emma called. "No fair. I was just telling Nick how much you liked me, and now you're abandoning me?"

"You're in safe hands," she called back, then caught Nick's gaze as he turned to walk with her. "Safety in numbers."

"As in, Chaz was alone when he went off the bridge," Nick said softly.

Sarah nodded. "I'm glad I didn't have to figure out how to sneak my Smith & Wesson into the hospital, but I wish I had it with me, anyway."

"We'll follow Dad's truck. Gerard carries his weapon and keeps it locked in his console when he's in a no-weapon zone."

"I still don't want Edward to drive back alone." She glanced over her shoulder toward Gerard's vehicle. "Sounds like you'll have a struggle to manage two words with Emma. Listen to her chattering to Gerard." She paused as the rise and fall of Emma's soliloquy reached them. "She sounds the way Dad used to when he drank too much coffee."

Nick placed an arm around Sarah, and it felt natural, the way it used to feel when they were kids walking home from a fishing expedition or cave exploration and he just casually rested his forearm on her shoulder. Like buddies.

"Think there's any way to keep Emma handcuffed to the house for the next couple of months?" he asked. "Reinjury is much more dangerous than the first injury."

Sarah looked up at him as they neared Dad's pickup. "Keeping that child still is like trying to keep a chrysalis from bursting into a butterfly."

Nick couldn't prevent a smile. "Isn't that exactly what she's doing? I'm surprised the two of you get along so well—she's so much like Shelby."

There was a short, thoughtful pause. "We've always been very close. I lived at home while I attended university at Cape Girardeau, so I spent as much time as I could with her in the evenings, even after I graduated and got a job."

"And Shelby? Wasn't she ever in Emma's life?"

"Oh, she made a good babysitter every so often, and she loves Emma, of course, but after high school she wasn't home much. She met a guy at a youth rally who wanted to be a missionary, so she attended

College of the Ozarks, worked her way through and got married. She's never looked back."

He studied Sarah. "And yet you stayed in the same town with your family. You were always the independent one, and you didn't take off and fly like your sister."

Sarah shrugged. "I guess dreams change."

"Your dream was to be a famous novelist and travel the world."

"Emma's my top priority, so some other things might have to fall by the wayside to get her raised."

"I'll have a talk with her on the drive," Nick promised. "Even if I have to raise my voice to get her to shut up for a few minutes. Maybe it's a good idea that you don't go with us, after all. That way she might be more likely to listen to me as a doctor. It's vital that she realizes how dangerous a head injury can be."

"And while you're at it, tell her about Chaz."

Nick nodded. "Convince her how serious this whole situation is."

"She needs to know she's not invincible."

"I'll make sure of it."

"If she was attacked, her attacker's going to do all it takes to keep her from recalling what she might have seen." Sarah's voice trembled.

Nick gave in to instinct and wrapped his arms around her. It began as a simple attempt to comfort her, but when she stayed there, and pressed her forehead against his chest, the comforting touch became a hug. And so much more. Why had the Russells moved away? Why hadn't Sarah stayed in Jolly Mill, the way she was supposed to? Nothing had happened the way it should have.

Dad came at last. Nick caught his gaze and saw a half grin and raised eyebrow as Dad unlocked the doors. Nick reluctantly opened the passenger door for Sarah.

She looked up and gave him a serene smile. "Thanks, Nick. I think you're my hero."

"You think?" he teased.

She chuckled as she stepped into the truck. He closed the door and stood looking at her. His admiration soared. Granted, when they were sixteen, she'd had no choice but to go with her parents, but what if he'd followed up on an urge that had haunted him since the day the Russell family left for St. Louis? What if he'd looked her up after graduation? What if they'd reconnected? Would he be a divorced man now, or would he have married the right woman in the first place—his best friend?

Edward slid behind the steering wheel of his elderly pickup truck and reached across to pat Sarah's hand. "Playing bodyguard?"

"I thought you'd be less likely to be run off the road by some maniac if they saw two people through the rearview window instead of one."

"You realize Gerard's planning to follow me home, anyway."

She did. And she felt like a hypocrite for not telling her beloved "second father" the whole reason she wanted to ride with him. Oh, there were plenty of reasons. Some had to do with not wanting to spend so much time with Nick right now, because her emotions were running so high, and because she tingled from head to foot any time he touched her, even accidentally. What an unexpected shock that had been—old feelings for him resurfacing after all this time.

She also, suddenly, inexplicably, wanted Nick to spend more time with his daughter without the birth mother running interference. Give him a chance to warm up to her before discovering she was his. Now that Sarah had decided to tell everyone the truth, she wanted it to be a happy truth, one Nick might even welcome in time.

Edward pulled out of the hospital parking lot and drove down Euclid. A glance in the rearview mirror showed that, indeed, Gerard was following them, and several cars also trailed his SUV. Unless the killer wanted a dozen witnesses, he would not be attacking anyone with a car on this trip.

"She's going to be okay, you know," Edward said.

Sarah swallowed, thinking about those scrapbooks and old-fashioned picture albums Mom had so lovingly used to frame the adorable antics and accomplishments throughout Emma's life, from birth to three weeks ago.

John wouldn't be here until later this evening, and Sarah needed those books now. She wanted to share them with Edward, enjoy them with him, and she desperately needed him to forgive her for the tragedy she'd caused—for his loss, for Aunt Peg's loss. Would he ever forgive her or her parents for robbing them of the opportunity of watching their granddaughter grow up?

She needed to turn each page for Edward, tell Emma's story, explain everything. Selfish? Yes. How badly she needed him standing beside her when she broke the news to Nick, and especially to Emma. Would they be devastated? Would they be shocked? Angry? Shouldn't she wait until all this danger was ended before sharing this secret? How could she place this distraction in their way?

And yet, in the midst of his grief, Edward could receive such hope. New life. A fresh outlook.

"I mean it, Sarah Fey," Edward said. "She's one of our own. We protect our own, no matter what."

Sarah swallowed, thinking of Aunt Peg. No one had been able to protect her. "Only God can do that for sure, Edward."

"But I believe God brought you here for a reason." He eased his foot against the brake at a stop sign and turned right, then almost immediately left again.

Sarah glanced at him. He was a strong man with

powerful arms, a strong jawline and a piercing stare that telegraphed well from the pulpit. Nick looked so much like his father. "I think you're right." She swallowed hard through a dry throat. "My cousin John is coming. He should be here long before dark—I couldn't stop him this time. I think he plans to try establishing a homegrown police force."

"I'd join that force it if meant protecting those I love."

"I know you would." She stared down at the train tracks as they drove over the bridge. "He's also bringing some old-fashioned photo albums and scrapbooks."

Edward glanced at her, his thick eyebrows raised. "That'll be nice to see, but any specific reason he's going out of his way for family pictures right now?"

"I asked him to. I thought you might enjoy them."

"Since you're staying with Carmen, why don't we let John stay at my place?"

"Thanks. I'm sure he'd appreciate it. He wants to be close, and he'll probably want to take a turn on guard duty."

Edward had his signal on and was turning right onto the highway when a low-slung gray car raced through the intersection, ignoring the red light. It cut in front of them closely enough Sarah squeezed her eyes shut, expecting the screech of metal against metal. Edward slammed the brake and instinctively slung his right arm in front of her, despite the seat belt. She held her breath to keep from crying out.

They most definitely were still on edge.

"Okay, honey?"

She opened her eyes, took note of the car's license plate number, took a breath. "Fine. You?"

"Just hot under the collar."

"Where are the police when you need them?"

He chuckled. "At least Monett *has* a police force."

Her cell phone beeped. She pulled it from her pocket and answered to the background sound of Emma's raised, angry voice and Gerard's deep, soothing tones.

"Did you catch the license plate?" Nick asked.

She recited the letters and numbers she'd automatically memorized.

"Good girl. You haven't lost your touch."

"Calm Emma down."

"Will do, but first I need to call that license plate into the city police so we can get the number on record."

"Just in case, huh? You know they'll be out of city limits before anyone could catch them."

"Doesn't matter. A record's a record. Might come in handy later. You and Dad okay?"

"We're fine. The world is filled with rotten drivers, but not every one of them is a killer. Let's try not to freak out again before we make it home. Sounds like Emma's reached her limit for the day."

"I can't wait for her to meet Carmen's Nina. That'll calm her right down."

"Good, then start talking about her right now. And tell her our cousin John will be here tonight."

"He doesn't think we can protect her?"

"He likes to be in the middle of all the action. He's driving from Sikeston. See you in a few." She disconnected.

Edward pulled onto the lane behind the crazy driver and picked up speed, taking obvious care not to get too close, even though the car had slowed down considerably. It turned at the next traffic signal, and Sarah noted that Edward's hands relaxed their grip on the steering wheel.

"We're definitely all too overwhelmed," he said. "This killer obviously doesn't use the same M.O. every time, which has Gerard concerned."

"I don't mind a little hyper-alertness right now, but it doesn't feel too great, does it?"

Edward gave a long, tired sigh. His whole body seemed to slump. "Not a lot feels too great right now, sweetheart. For either of us."

She glanced at him. Could he handle more? When she was growing up, she used to believe Edward Tyler, like her own father, could shoulder all the world's problems with a gentle smile and a calm word for anyone who needed it. He lived to help others. He lived to serve God. Right now, looking at him, she saw only hollowed-out eyes and a sagging face. Losing Aunt Peg had destroyed the outward joy that had always been a part of his personality. Would learning he had a grandchild bring him some new life, or would knowing he'd missed out on sixteen years place a fresh break in his heart?

TEN

The beauty of southern Missouri's green forest and golden pastures on rolling hills raced past the perimeter of Nick's vision as he focused on the pickup ahead of them, on Sarah's profile. It appeared as if she and Dad were deep in conversation. Unlike in this SUV, where Emma had stolen the show and most of the oxygen in her efforts to wind down from the excitement of the day, Dad seemed to be allowed a chance to contribute to the conversation.

"…never even dated in high school, unlike Shelby, according to Mom, who practically had a date every night. Sarah still doesn't date much. She even lived at home with us while she was in college. She had a lot of friends, and some of them were guys, but I never noticed her spending more time with one than any other."

"She doesn't seem shy." Gerard was obviously drawing Emma out, encouraging her to talk about her sister—probably to calm her down, although he'd picked up on Nick's interest in Sarah almost immediately at the hospital. Maybe he was trying to give Nick a chance to be filled in on the past few years of her life.

"Mom called her self-possessed," Emma said.

Nick smiled. That was Sarah. Calm, a good conversationalist when circumstances called for it, but unlike Emma, who used her hands as much as her mouth and facial expression to communicate, Sarah thought before she spoke. Serenity was part of her nature. It didn't appear as if there were any silences in the cab of Dad's truck right now, however. It was obvious from the nodding and frequent presentation of Sarah's side profile that they weren't lacking subjects to discuss.

"I mean, really, Mom and Dad and John and practically all our cousins in Sikeston have tried to set her up with one guy or another, but she's so particular. One guy lived too far away, and one was too hung up on his car, and the one guy she actually did date in college who asked her to marry him? She flat turned him down. He wanted to move to St. Louis after graduation, and she hates St. Louis. I mean, really? If you love a guy, don't you want to be where he is? I don't think she loved him." With a slightly wobbly voice, Emma crossed her arms over her chest and stared out the side window. "Mom and Dad always worried about her." Her voice had softened considerably. "She's always been, like, my best friend? And all my friends at school think it's kind of great? But I know our parents worried about her. And now she's stuck with me. They would be so upset by that."

"Stuck?" Nick chuckled. "Does she behave as if she feels she's stuck with you?"

"Well, no, but—"

"And she's always been this way? Spent a lot of time with you?"

"Yeah, but—"

"How long did it take her to come after you when she found out you left Sikeston?"

"I know what you're saying, but—"

"What's changed?"

Emma sighed and fell silent for a precious few seconds, staring out the side window. "Besides Mom and Dad being gone forever?"

"I mean between Sarah and you. You behave as if you're being forced into her life."

"I am."

"Doesn't look that way to me. Can't you see how crazy she is about you?"

"But now we can't be best friends anymore. She has to be my guardian."

"I know how you could help her out with that," Gerard said. "Don't act out, so she doesn't have anything to guard. You could be more like roommates."

Nick suppressed a snort. "Oh, sure, like that's a possibility."

Emma shot Nick a glare over her shoulder, then

winced when she turned too quickly. "Hey, I'm not… I mean, I don't… It isn't as if I make a habit of acting out, you know. I go to church, I'm not into drugs, I don't smoke. I had a taste of beer once— but don't tell Sarah—and I nearly barfed, so that's out. I—"

"You sound like a poster child for good behavior," Nick said. "I guess that means you're not going to fly into another snit and come racing across the state again without telling your sister."

"But that's different—"

"Nothing different about it, sweetheart," Gerard said. "That's the kind of behavior that'll shorten your sister's life and place an unbearable burden on her shoulders, so if you care at all about her, you'll start behaving like a godly young woman who honors her parents. Now, in the eyes of the law, that means Sarah."

"And as soon as your cousin John arrives from Sikeston this evening," Nick said, "you can honor him the same way."

Emma gasped and would have done a 180 if her seat belt hadn't jerked her up short. She winced again and grabbed at her bandaged head. "John's coming?"

"After today's excitement? He doesn't want Sarah to have to deal with this alone, and he has to see for himself you're okay."

"Cool!"

Nick deflated. What he wanted was for her to realize how much danger her policeman cousin thought she could be in.

"Carmen told me Kirstie Marshal's daughter, Lynley, is coming to town tonight," Emma said. "She's single, too, and so wants a man. John's a perfect guy to get married and treat a lady like she deserves to be treated. He's always been so good to Sarah, trying to set her up with his friends, and then trying again when she keeps turning down all second dates. John could put up with any woman; he's used to Sarah, who ignores his help. We need to make sure they meet."

"John and Sarah?" Gerard's voice was as dry as the dirt roads that led from Highway 60.

"No, silly, John and Lynley."

Nick sighed and met Gerard's gaze in the rearview mirror. "I don't think you're grasping the seriousness of the situation you're in, little girl."

"I'm not a little girl. And I've learned a valuable lesson. If I'm going to be eligible for sports next fall, I have to take it easy all summer."

"That's it?" Gerard asked.

"And if I give Sarah another scare like the one I did coming here, I'll be grounded for life."

"I'll see to it, but even that's not good enough," Nick said. "The point you need to grasp is that there's a killer who might well believe you can identify him."

"Well, would you please spread the word that I can't remember? Maybe he'll take the hint and go away."

"If you'd recognized him, he'd be in jail, and even the stupidest of killers would realize that already," Gerard said. "His goal is to stop you from remembering."

"You could get your memory back at any time." Nick leaned forward until he caught Emma's attention. "Most people are smart enough to know that."

"You're a target, kiddo," Gerard said.

Some of the color left her cheeks. "But why would a killer hang around Jolly Mill? Why not just disappear?"

"Because leaving now—especially if he's a longtime resident—would only draw attention to him."

"Now you see why Sarah's so frightened?" Gerard caught Nick's gaze again and nodded.

Emma slumped in her seat and covered her face with her hands. "My poor sister. If not for me, she wouldn't be here. She'd be hiding out in her house working on her latest novel when she's not swamped with lesson plans."

Nick smiled to himself. "She started writing articles for the school paper our freshman year. I know she loves to write, but you're more important to her than writing or being famous or traveling the world."

Emma blinked. "She said that?"

"Sure did. I can't see Sarah seeking fame, anyway. She's not that type."

"But I'm stopping her from her dream."

"Nothing's stopping her. In fact, having you with her might even inspire her."

"Sure thing," Gerard said. "Especially if you're willing to help out around the house so she'll have time to write after work."

"I could totally do that, but do you know how hard it is to work a full-time job, then come home and—"

"And see the house cleaned by her mature younger sister, who has dinner waiting?" Gerard asked. "Then you could ace your homework to get a scholarship to college while Sarah writes. You're not a baby in diapers."

Something caught Emma's attention past the fence to their right. She jerked forward in her seat, once again catching herself in the seat belt. She pointed out the window. "Pine!" she shrieked.

To his credit, Gerard didn't swerve. Nick had learned enough after less than twenty-four hours with Emma to realize their subject had once more changed, and in her overly excited state, one had to be prepared for anything. He waited.

She turned around, her mouth a round O, her white teeth peeping out. "There was a piney scent, too. I remember now. Citrus-pine and cinnamon."

"The aroma at the hospital?" Gerard asked. "You just now remembered that?"

"I caught the scent at the conference center. The cinnamon could've been from Parker's Diner, sure, but why did I smell it in the hospital?"

"Maybe because Billy came to the hospital to see how you were?" Nick asked. "And Gerard was trimming trees this morning, weren't you, Gerard? Alec said he couldn't find you, and you had sawdust on your clothes when you came to give us a ride to the hospital."

The big man groaned. "Juniper trees. That would contribute the pine scent."

"You didn't take time to change."

Gerard leaned over for Emma to catch a whiff of his shirt. "Ignore the sweat. Familiar?"

She giggled, then sniffed his shirt. "Maybe, if you were trimming juniper trees. But the berries are used in soaps and stuff, and they have a citrus-pine scent, too. What if I was smelling somebody's soap?"

Nick frowned. "Maybe. Or the scent clue could be a dead end."

"I'm not ruling it out yet," Gerard said. "Emma, any more memories?"

"You mean since you asked me ten minutes ago? No."

"Why didn't you enter the building?" Nick asked.

Emma fell silent and sat back in her seat. "How do you know I didn't?"

"There was mud all around the building from

recent rains. Sarah and I tracked it into the building, but ours were the only footprints."

Emma covered her face with her hands and released a heavy sigh. "I wish I could remember something. Anything."

Nick grimaced. Someone else was likely wishing just as heartily that she never would.

"You change your name to Atlas lately?" Edward's voice broke into Sarah's internal debate. "You look like someone who's trying to carry the world on your shoulders."

"Would the responsibility for one sixteen-year-old count? One who never sits still, never thinks before she acts, who thinks she's on her own now that Mom and Dad are gone?" How badly she wanted to dump all her pent-up frustrations on Edward. And how badly he needed to be protected from those frustrations.

But really? Did Edward need protection? Maybe he was in need of hope.

It was far past time to tell him everything. He deserved to know he had a granddaughter. That he was family. Sarah's heart rate crept up, and the cab of the truck began to feel a little too warm. "You and Aunt Peg and Mom and Dad were the best of friends before we left here."

"That we were."

"It's my fault your friendship was damaged after we moved."

He shot her a quick look of surprise. "First of all, what makes you think our friendship was damaged? Second, how could anything like that have been your fault?"

Sarah hesitated. "We only moved across the state, not the other side of the world. I know you and Aunt Peg must have been shocked when you found out about Emma nine months after we left Jolly Mill."

"Shocked? No way. Lives get complicated. We knew Mark and Lydia wanted another child and were thrilled when we heard about Emma."

"I remember when you visited. But weren't you disappointed they didn't tell you before she was born?"

For a moment, he was silent. "Adoptions aren't the same as carrying a baby to term." He glanced at her, appearing confused. "We knew that, and we understood their wish to keep the adoption quiet. No one heard it from our lips. Not even Nick. He was buried in preparations for scholarships and premed studies then, anyway."

Adoption. "They told you."

"Um, Sarah, there's a fly buzzing around in this cab somewhere. You probably should close your mouth. What's the big deal?"

Surprise held her speechless for a moment as they drove past a pond filled with cattle. Obviously, the afternoon had turned out hotter than a typical day in May. Taking note of the weather was on the bottom of her priority list.

"There's something else on your mind," Edward said. "Your eyes are about to bug out of their sockets, and you're trying to tie a knot in some of your fingers."

She glanced down at her hands and flattened them on her knees. "Oh, Edward, you don't know how much we missed you and Aunt Peg and Nick when we went to St. Louis. At one point I begged Dad to let us move back." And that was before Emma was born, when the whole truth would have come out. She hadn't cared.

"Things changed for everyone then, sweetheart, but your dad couldn't keep working a full-time job at the hospital plus pastor the church. It got to be too much for him. He thought giving up nursing and becoming a hospital chaplain would give him the break he needed to spend more time with his family."

"It didn't work out. He missed church work."

"I knew he would. All they wanted was for you and Shelby to have the best life had to offer. What was the desire of your heart, Sarah Fey?"

"I always wanted to return to Jolly Mill."

"And yet you stayed in Sikeston and took a job after college."

"I couldn't leave Emma." The words were out before she considered them, and she felt Edward's sudden interest. Siblings didn't hang around home just to be close to their younger brothers or sisters, especially after graduating from college.

She took a slow, deep breath and gathered strength from the bucolic scene of cattle and horses and the occasional llama grazing around ponds and among huge round bales of hay.

"If there's something you need to talk about, sweetheart, you know I'm here for you."

She leaned forward and glanced in the side mirror. A convoy continued to follow them as they passed the intersection of state highways 60 and 97. She knew she should tell Nick first. Everything Sarah could recall from that murky night told her that he was Emma's father, and his words today had confirmed it, but she couldn't suppress the fear she felt at the thought. What would his reaction be? Selfishly, she needed to know she wouldn't be alone, but she also wanted Edward to know now that he had a grandchild, to ease the lines of pain around his eyes. "Mom and Dad didn't lie to you. They adopted Emma, but they did it because she was their granddaughter."

There was a long silence. The truck tires rumbled loudly on the shoulder before correcting.

Sarah glanced at Edward. "Now who's catching flies?"

He closed his mouth.

"You know that party Nora had at her place just before we left?" she asked.

"You think anyone's ever going to forget it? That turned into a nightmare for poor Nora."

Sarah grimaced. "It was an awful thing for someone to do to her."

"And to the kids."

"Did anyone ever find out who would spike the soda with ecstasy? Or why?"

Edward shook his head. "Nora hired a private investigator. She and Kirstie Thompson and Carmen scoured the town for clues—and to be honest, those three ladies could probably start their own investigative service. No one ever found out who drugged the kids. There were a lot of guesses, but no answers."

"Shelby was so excited about the party, but it turned out she was sick that night."

He glanced at her. "Nora had to give the sheriff a list of names of the teenagers at the party. Shelby's name was there. Yours wasn't."

"I dropped the costume for the night, so Carmen mistook me for Shelby. Everybody did."

He raised his eyebrows. "That was unusual."

"I was so devastated about our upcoming move to St. Louis that I decided since Shelby wasn't going I would take her place. I wore her clothes and undid the Goth. In the dark, no one could tell the difference, because I'd washed the black stuff out of my hair and actually put her makeup on instead of my own."

"And if she hadn't been sick?"

"I probably wouldn't have gone to say goodbye the way I wanted to, and maybe, just maybe, she would have been the one to drink that drug and end up pregnant. And she wouldn't still be judging me after all these years." Not that Sarah would wish that on her sister, but it might teach Shelby a little compassion.

"Judging you? Why?"

"I sullied the Russell name, even though no one knows Emma's mine except Mom, Dad, Shelby and my cousin John Fred."

"Honey, you were raped."

Sarah looked down and saw that she was trying to tie her fingers into knots once again. This was going to be even harder than she'd thought. "How can you say I was raped? How can anyone say that for sure? We were all raped that night by the twisted person who drugged us."

"But you were innocent."

"Then so was the father. If I'd been perfectly innocent I wouldn't have acted on a wrong impulse. I also wouldn't have pretended to be someone I wasn't."

Despite the serious conversation, Edward chuckled. "Dressed normally, with your natural hair, is it possible you were trying to reveal your real self to your friends in Jolly Mill before you left?"

Sarah sat back, trying hard to reject the old ooze of guilt that attempted to cover her once more. She considered his words. "I had an agenda, Edward."

"You sure?"

"Okay, it wasn't totally that." She swallowed. "But you and Aunt Peg knew how much I loved Nick."

The silence lingered. The center line passed her vision at hypnotically increasing speed. She'd finally given Edward the clue he needed to work things out for himself, and she could hear his breathing grow unsteady.

A loud swallow echoed through the cab. "Nick."

"He was the one I went to say goodbye to, and I went without the Goth getup because he'd told me once he had a crush on Shelby. I wanted so badly to be her, and to be the one he loved. I thought a goodbye kiss—"

"He never loved your sister, Sarah. One short two-week crush at most? I think he was simply imagining you without the glop on your face and hair. His silly crush on Shelby was nothing compared to the lasting love you and Nick shared, that powerful bond of friendship that Peg kept telling me would blossom into enduring love." Poor Edward's voice had begun to quiver.

She quietly caught her breath and allowed a smile to spread across her face. "You really think so?"

"You know the truth. It was always you and Nick, from grade school on. Peg and I hoped you two would remain friends and eventually get married. We both ached for you and Nick when Mark took that job in St. Louis. Nick wasn't the same after you left, but he plunged into extra studies, volunteering at the hospital, earning that scholarship."

"If only we'd known," she whispered. "I can't tell you without a doubt that Nick is Emma's father, because I don't remember—the drug, you know. I have no actual memories to back it up, but looking at her I see so much of Nick, of you, of Aunt Peg."

There was a long silence, and then a deep sigh. "So you're saying Peg and I have...a granddaughter?"

Something dripped on Sarah's hand, and she looked down, startled to see that she was crying. Again. Where had all these tears come from lately? "Nick's the only one I went to see that night. So many times, I'd look at him and wonder if he was thinking of Shelby. That was why I couldn't resist pretending to be her that night. I wanted to be close to him. I told myself I didn't care if he did think he was kissing Shelby, but I did. Today he told me without realizing it that he shares some of the same memories."

The truck slowed just a little, and that was when Sarah realized the fence posts on each side of the road were a blur, and the truck was shaking.

"I thought you said you didn't remember what happened."

"I don't recall much, but I do remember I went looking for Nick after I got my soda. I didn't even realize anything had happened—I mean, I don't remember a kiss or anything. Three months later I found out I was pregnant."

"Do you remember finding Nick at the party?"

"Yes, but sometimes I wondered if it was because I wanted to remember. Everyone wanted to talk to me because they thought I was Shelby. I've carried a few images of Nick sitting on a square bale of hay in the loft above everyone else."

"It's something he would do."

"Yes, but I knew that about him, too. By that time things were hazy. Mom and Dad never knew my suspicions about Nick being Emma's father. How could I do that to him?"

"You thought you were doing the right thing, as your parents did."

"They convinced me to let them adopt Emma because I had my whole life ahead of me, and they wanted me to live it, and they didn't want Emma to live with the stigma of illegitimacy. They thought it was such an awful thing to happen to me, I couldn't tell them I thought the father might be Nick, because according to their reactions, it would have ruined his life."

"How I wish we'd caught the nasty piece of work

who did this to us all." Edward's voice was suddenly gravelly with unaccustomed anger.

Sarah sighed and leaned her head against the seat. "If that night hadn't happened we wouldn't have Emma," she said quietly.

"You haven't told Nick?"

She shook her head. "I can't help wondering what it might do to him."

"You don't have the luxury of time now, honey. He needs to know."

"Yes."

Edward took her by the arm and squeezed it briefly, then returned his hand to the steering wheel. "I don't think you understand, sweetheart. I'm not just saying that it's the right thing to do—which it is. I'm saying that for Nick to discover he has a daughter and that you're the mother of that daughter and that his whole world hasn't been destroyed because of the works of wicked, greedy people these past years, it might counteract the blackness that's bearing down on him right now."

Sarah glanced in the rearview mirror again, and though the reflection was too small for her to see Nick sitting alone in the backseat, she ached for the pain he'd endured. "I'm so sorry he's had such a nightmarish life. He didn't deserve it."

"You're sure he's Emma's father, aren't you?"

"Until today I told myself maybe it was wishful thinking, but after Nick shared his memories...yes.

This morning he asked me if Shelby was Emma's mother, and Alec remarked that Emma looks just like Aunt Peg did at sixteen."

Sarah didn't realize until too late that they'd sped past the turn-off to Jolly Mill and that the truck was once more quaking at a frightening speed. "Edward, you'd better pull over and let me drive."

"I'm fine."

"Your truck isn't, and you just found out you might be a grandfather, so I don't think you're fine, either."

He glanced at the speedometer and lifted his foot from the accelerator once again. "Peg and I thought we'd never be grandparents. How I wish she could have lived to see this day."

Sarah blinked, staring straight ahead.

"Peg would have been wildly in love with our granddaughter."

Of course she would have. Why couldn't Sarah have seen that sooner?

"I can tell you this—my granddaughter will have the protection of a full army if it comes to that." Edward spared a look for Sarah as the truck slowed and the steering wheel stopped vibrating. "And I have a powerful impression that our lives will never be the same."

ELEVEN

"What on earth is Edward doing up there?" Emma cried. "Is he sick? Did he have a stroke? He passed the Jolly Mill sign. Isn't that the turn-off?" She swiveled in her seat and looked behind them, then winced again and touched her head. "Looks like we're all still following him, though. Want to call and see what's up?"

"Sit back in your seat and stop trying to pop your head off." Nick had Sarah on his cell within seconds. "Mind giving us an update?"

"All is…uh, well. Edward and I had a lot to catch up on and we kind of lost track of time and mileage."

"Ya think?"

"Relax, it's okay now." She chuckled, but the sound was a bit forced. "You know what an exciting conversationalist I am, and I distracted Edward from the road for a moment. We'll take the next turn. See you at Carmen's."

She disconnected, and he folded his phone,

attempting to decipher what it was he'd heard in her voice. Anxiety? Fear?

"Well?" Emma asked.

"Sarah said they got distracted, deep in conversation."

"Does your father have a habit of speeding and missing his turns?" Gerard asked.

"First time for everything." Nick studied the silhouettes in the truck ahead of them. "Emma, don't do this kind of thing to your sister again. Or to my father. Sounds like you've managed to freak them both out."

"Me? You're blaming me for Edward nearly running off the road and missing his turn at a gazillion miles an hour?" Emma turned in her seat again, this time much more slowly. Her scowl didn't go very deep, and it didn't reach her eyes. "Anyway, he'd better be careful. That truck already looks like it's about to take its final breath." Her eyes widened and her lips parted. "You know what? I do remember you and Sarah calling my name when I was at the conference center this morning."

Again the subject change. A person could get whiplash trying to keep up with her. "Of course you did, and you didn't answer because you thought we'd make you come back."

"No, that's not—"

"Did it occur to you that we would have joined you? That Sarah was simply worried about your safety?"

"But things happened so quickly, and you've seen how overprotective Sarah is."

"With good reason. While we were at Parker's looking for you, Sarah got a call from your cousin John. Remember Chaz? Someone ran him off the road into Spring River. He's dead."

Gerard sucked in his breath. "Man, way to scare the poor child to death."

Nick couldn't miss Emma's reaction. Her skin paled for the second time on this short drive. Her brown eyes stared ahead on the road. "I'm not a... a child." Her voice was barely there. "W-when?"

"Some fishermen found him this morning. Dad's already been to see his parents."

A look of shock spread across Emma's face, and Nick was sorry he'd been so abrupt with her.

Gerard glanced around at Nick. "I need to have a talk with Edward, then."

"I'm sure he didn't interrogate them. He was there to comfort them."

"Then they're the ones I should visit. They'll want to know who did this to their son, because I can almost guarantee that's who killed the others. And don't worry, I'll be gentle."

"Sounds like he wasn't much older than me." Emma's voice had suddenly gone hoarse. "Chaz? He was only what, twenty-something?" Tears slid down her white cheeks. "How could someone do that?"

Nick hesitated. Sarah was right; this overly sheltered girl needed to be shocked enough that she would stay out of trouble. From what he'd heard so far, she'd been basically raised by three parents, plus a very protective cousin. A kid would have to develop a strong sense of independence just to stand on her own two feet. This one had that quality flowing out her ears.

He hadn't realized how awful it would feel to shock her out of her sense of security, though. If only he hadn't been forced to destroy the innocent faith of a child who believed in the goodness of all mankind.

"The person who slaughtered our friends and loved ones is a monster in disguise, Emma," Gerard said gently, before Nick could say anything. "Not all humans are like your family or mine, and as you mature you have to learn that ugly fact."

She hugged herself, shoulders slumping forward. "It's working."

"No going outside alone," Nick said. "And especially no running off like you did this morning."

"I know. I get it. But who can we trust?" She wiped at her face, mingling tears with purple mascara. She made Nick want to wrap his arms around her and promise no one would ever hurt her again.

"You have a whole town full of protectors," Nick said. "But we can't be sure which ones are the protectors and which one of all those good people might want to hurt you. Unless you're with Sarah, Gerard,

Edward or several of our other very close friends, you mustn't allow yourself to be alone with anyone until we've found our killer."

"I'm not taking anybody to the bathroom with me."

Nick met Gerard's gaze in the rearview mirror and shared a hesitant grin. What would it take to quell this girl's spirit? "Okay, but only at Carmen's. And I've already warned you not to bump your head again for six months, right?"

"I don't plan to bump it at all."

"Doesn't matter whether you plan to or not," Nick said. "Life doesn't always work out the way we—"

Emma gasped. "I remember something else! The cellar? Where I fell? I heard footsteps going down there when I was on the other side of the building talking to God about my parents. That's why I didn't answer when you two shouted to me."

"What else do you remember?" Nick asked.

She closed her eyes and took a deep breath, as if willing her brain to lose that layer of fog that covered the most vital facts with many concussions. "I had to find out who was there, of course."

"Of course," Gerard said dryly.

Nick groaned. Even after she'd been convinced enough about her parents' murders to drive all the way across the state to help "investigate," she thought she was indestructible.

"You screamed," Nick said. "Sarah and I heard you on our way up the hillside."

"I don't remember that, but I'm pretty sure someone was in the cellar."

Nick closed his eyes. "Gerard—"

"Got it. I'll check the cellar for footprints."

"Emma, you didn't see anyone? Hear a voice?"

"I think that's where I smelled that scent. The cinnamon and pine."

"In the cellar?"

"I think so. I'm sorry, I just don't remember more."

"Until you do, and until we can catch whoever you saw, you're under the protective custody of your friends," Nick said. "Poor Carmen's going to have an unexpected party at her house tonight."

Gerard glanced over his shoulder at Nick. "She likes parties. Soon as I drop you two off I'll do some tracking around the conference building, see if I can find something useful, talk to the Collinses, try to talk to the sheriff again."

"Alec can help," Nick said. "I know you two clash like stainless-steel cymbals, but you need to work together right now if we're going to prevent this killer from getting away with…more."

Sarah's hands ached from clenching them together so tightly on their highway race, but the narrow country road onto which they'd turned had ensured that Edward would keep the speed to an acceptable level. They would reach Jolly Mill in another moment or two.

There was no missing the excitement in Edward's demeanor, and she was glad she'd told him, despite her ridiculous timing.

"Edward, as you and Dad have always preached, we don't have automatic protection from all evil in this world," she said.

He shot her a smile. "Mark and I have also preached that God will repay us for the years the locusts have eaten. Emma's that repayment for me, and she will be for Nick."

"You're truly happy about this shock I've dumped on you?"

"You're the wordsmith, sweetheart—what's a more powerful word than ecstatic? Renewed? Hopeful?"

How she loved this man. "You know all those times you and Aunt Peg asked for me to come stay with you for the summer all through the remainder of my school years?"

"Sure do. I finally understand why you didn't."

"I couldn't leave Emma that long. And I really wanted to see you, but then as Emma developed, and, to me, at least, began to look more and more like her father. I couldn't take the chance that I'd let something slip. Nick was in college, then med school, and I was young enough to be afraid that if he discovered he had a daughter, he might chuck it all to take on his fatherly duties. We had friends who'd had babies and dropped out of school. I know I was young and more than a little paranoid, but Mom and Dad had made a huge impression on me about having a baby out of wedlock and ruining our lives." She stared out at the corn growing in the field to her right. "In trying to protect Nick, I robbed you and Aunt Peg and Nick of the joy of watching Emma grow up."

Edward sighed. "Is there any way you could look at this situation without taking on the responsibility for the whole world? Can't you see that you were caught by the wiles of a drug pusher, and only that? You and your family made the best decisions you knew to make, and together you've raised a beautiful girl who has a heart filled with innocence and love. I can't help believing God had a hand in bringing her here. He simply used her strong spirit."

"You mean her stubbornness. She got that from me. I do wish Aunt Peg could have known her."

"But you know she will someday. Let's just make sure that's a long time from now."

Sarah had always loved Edward's calm patience and loving attitude. "I wish I could have proof about Nick's paternity before I dump this on him."

"I already do."

"I mean positive proof. We could have blood

tests or something. After all these years of believing, what if I've been wrong?"

"You think Nick's memories, which are totally separate from yours, are also wrong? Get serious, honey. I know it with every part of my being." He slowed and turned onto his street. "The minute you told me what happened, I realized the truth. It's been staring me in the face all these years, especially when I saw my granddaughter in the flesh last night, sitting on the sofa next to her father. It amazes me that Peg and I didn't see it all these years when your parents sent us family pictures." He pulled into the driveway and parked. "Let's get Emma's fifteen suitcases repacked and haul them over to Carmen's." He started to climb from the truck.

Sarah placed a hand on his arm and glanced out the rear window, where Gerard had pulled up behind them. "Edward, you're the first person I've told about Emma. Would you give me time to work up the nerve to tell Nick and Emma?"

"You know I will, but why should you have to carry the whole burden now? I'm here for you. You know that, don't you? Isn't that why you came to me first? Let me help you shoulder this load."

She'd allowed the complications in her life to be carried by others for far too long. "I have to be the one to break it to them, but if you'll help me with the fallout—"

"I'll be here." He patted her cheek. "We've always

been family, haven't we? That's more of a reality than ever before."

Before she could reply, the passenger door swung open wide. "Dad, what on earth?" It was Nick.

"Hold it." Sarah turned to slide out, forcing Nick to step back. "That was my fault, so don't get all freaky, okay? I distracted Edward with stories from…home."

"You have got to be kidding me." Emma stepped around Nick, her hair in tangles around her bandage. "Whatever happens at home that's exciting enough to lead us on a high-speed chase down a two-lane highway?"

"Living with you is all the excitement anyone needs." Sarah grinned into her daughter's deep brown eyes—which really were just like Nick's. On instinct she caught Emma in a tight hug, enjoying the tickle of her child's long hair on her bare arm. "You know I love you, right?"

"Yeah, sis, and I'm not going to run off on you again, okay?" Emma's eyes were sparkling when she wriggled from Sarah's grasp. "I wish I'd gone with Edward. Nick and Gerard suddenly decided I needed a couple of dads on the drive from Monett. My ears are still ringing from all their fatherly advice."

"They're just men," Sarah said quietly. "They mean well."

Emma giggled. "Yeah, but if we'd switched, I might've stopped Edward from trying to blast off for the moon and you could have held hands with Nick in the backseat and made more gooey eyes at each other."

"*More* gooey eyes?" Nick caught her in an extremely gentle headlock and placed his knuckles to her scalp, threatening a noogie.

"Abuse! Abuse!" Emma cried. "I have a concussion!"

"Okay, that'll be enough arguing for a while." Edward came around the front of the truck and tugged his granddaughter away from his son, chuckling. He gazed down into her face as if she was a flawless diamond sparkling in the sun.

Emma returned the gaze with the same display of adoration. It seemed to Sarah as if the family recognition had taken place the first moment they saw one another last night.

And then Sarah glanced up at Nick, who watched his father and Emma, studying their faces, their eyes. He seemed unable to look away. In that moment, Sarah could almost visualize the whole truth filtering through him.

Sometime during that staring match she discovered that she was suddenly the object of Nick's focused attention. There was confusion in his eyes. As Gerard and Edward walked with Emma into the Tyler home to collect her things, Nick remained.

"Sarah. What's happening here?"

She focused on her breathing and willed her heart

rate to return to normal. "You asked me this morning if Shelby was Emma's birth mother. I didn't lie to you. She isn't. I just left out the rest of the story."

He took a deep breath and let it out. "Sarah," he whispered. "I believe I was *with* Shelby that night. Then nine months later there's a new child in the family? What was I supposed to believe?"

It was past time. "Shelby wasn't at the party. She spent the evening in the bathroom at home. I told you she was sick. That wasn't her you were with." He deserved the truth, and it wasn't going to be put off any longer. This was the whole reason she'd been afraid to come to Jolly Mill. "I decided to be Shelby that night. It was me. I'm Emma's mother."

He recoiled as if she'd just given him a hard punch in the gut. Cut to the core, she pivoted and started walking around the perimeter of the yard, just inside the shoulder-high shrubs that served as a fence.

"Sarah, please. Wait." He touched her shoulder.

She clenched her right fist as if she might slug him. Instead, she jerked from his touch and walked faster. Here she'd begun to believe what he and Edward had told her, that he'd never loved Shelby, but now he was obviously horrified to discover she, not Shelby, was the one he'd been with that night.

"Why is it so shocking to think that instead of with the ever popular Shelby Russell, you conceived a child with the ugly twin? What a sight I must have been compared to her. Me with my black clothing and black eyes, black hair. Was it so horrifying for you to—"

"Would you stop this? Sarah!"

She increased her pace.

"Sarah, you're wrong. Please stop and talk to me."

The wound she'd held deep inside for so many years ripped open once again. Everyone had loved Shelby, and Shelby had craved that love. For as long as Sarah could remember she'd sensed that need in her twin, and so she'd stood back, out of love for her sister, and allowed Shelby to receive what she craved, both at church and at school, and often at home, as well. Only when Sarah was with Edward and Aunt Peg, or fishing or hiking or exploring caves with Nick, did she feel free to open up and be herself.

"Honey, you aren't giving me a chance." Nick caught up with her. "I never dreamed that you... I didn't know you were there, that you were one of the victims."

"You think being that beautiful child's mother makes me a victim in any way?"

"No." His voice softened, gentled. "No way. Emma is nothing but a blessing. I'm sorry. It was a shock. That's all. I've been glad all these years that you didn't get drugged like the rest of us. Now to find out that you did... It took me by surprise. Please believe that if you believe nothing else."

She kept walking. The deepest pain she felt was

something she'd caused herself. She'd pretended to be Shelby, and it wasn't until she discovered she was pregnant that she realized Nick had accepted the advances from the person he thought was Shelby. That night, if nothing had happened and no one had drugged their sodas, she would have kissed him goodbye as Shelby and left that memory in his thoughts forever—not her, but Shelby. Despite what Edward said, and what he and Aunt Peg believed, Sarah knew she and Nick had never been anything but good buddies when she'd lived here—not in his eyes, anyway. Not then. There'd never been any romance between them.

Except now they had a child together, and she'd just finished telling him that, and she certainly hadn't received the response she'd hoped for.

She stopped so suddenly that Nick continued several feet before stopping and turning back. *Get the job done and get away from this situation as soon as possible.*

He heaved a deep breath. "You're as changeable as Emma." He grasped her gently by the shoulders, as if she might bolt again. "Listen to me, okay? Like everyone else, I don't have a lot of memories of the night of that party, but I do remember seeing who I *thought* was Shelby Russell coming toward me and sitting beside me on a bale of hay in the loft, and I thought about how strange that was, because she didn't usually waste her time on me. Later I thought that must have been part of the drug talking, because I knew that popular Shelby, who could get any guy she wanted, wouldn't be sitting beside me. By that time, I didn't want her to. I knew who I wanted beside me."

Sarah stopped breathing for a few seconds. She looked up at him. This was no time to get let emotions rule. "Let me guess," she said, trying to smile. "Petra Journigan." *Try to lighten the mood.* "She had a crush on you back then."

Nick grinned. But even that seemed wobbly, his breathing uneven. "Silly." He took her hand. "Want to walk some more? Only this time, a little slower?"

Sarah imagined tingles up her arm. *Let 'em tingle.* She needed time to decipher all he'd just told her, but for now, this was enough. So she walked beside him and enjoyed his touch.

"So, first of all, wow," he said as he tightened his hold gently.

She looked up at him.

"Emma. My child. Our child." He said the words reverently. "And that's what you were telling Dad about on the way here."

"Right." She felt warm all the way to her core. This was more what she'd hoped for.

"No wonder he lost control. That darling girl is ours? We made her?"

More than just tingles now. Far more. "I won't say for sure, because of the drug that night, but there was no one else I'd have wanted to be with, and you have some of the same memories." She listened to the sound of their footsteps, wondering if the senses she'd experienced today might dwell in her memories for the rest of her life.

"I'm not going to give in to instinct and run into the house and grab Emma up in my arms and hold her and welcome her to the family," Nick said. "But just so you know, that's what I want to do."

She smiled, but his words shot such warmth through her she wanted to cry. How well she understood that feeling.

"Just… Wow." He dashed the back of his hand across his face, and she saw a wet sparkle there. "This is like all the Christmases and birthdays I've ever had all rolled into one bundle of…total amazement."

"Thank You, God," she whispered, then more clearly, "You can't imagine how relieved I am to hear you say that."

"I want to tell the world that she's my daughter." He laughed with abandon. "Okay, I have so many questions, so many things I want to know. But first, why the pretense that night? Why did you make everyone believe you were Shelby?"

Sarah walked in silence for a few seconds. "Being Shelby that night gave me the courage to be more than just buddies with you. I know you didn't have a clue that I had a little crush on you."

A crush? Really? She'd given birth to his child and never seriously looked at another man since then. She was still withholding information.

His gaze gradually traveled to her face, his eyes filled with delight. "You came to the party for me that night?"

She nodded, looked away. "And then everything went so...crazy. I've always been pretty sure she was yours, but without recalling it all, I couldn't just flat-out say it's the truth until you told me what you did today. I couldn't incriminate you and ruin your career when you were just getting started."

He reached up and grasped her chin with both hands, as if he was holding something very precious. "After what Alec said about Mom's high school picture this morning, I couldn't help wondering. Hoping, Sarah."

Her throat tightened, but she swallowed back tears. There'd been enough tears.

"I just wanted to..." She closed her eyes. "I wanted to give you a simple goodbye kiss."

His hands closed around hers.

She opened her eyes. "I know I was just a kid and didn't know anything about love, but I knew how I felt about you, and I felt as if my heart was breaking, and you'd told me you liked Shelby...you know... that way. I didn't want to leave. I'd rather have died than leave Jolly Mill, but I never in a million years expected my actions would lead to pregnancy."

"How much do you actually remember?"

"Not enough. You?"

"I remembered a kiss, and brief flashes that have confused me for years, some of them so embarrassing I couldn't bring myself to tell my parents. When I heard about Emma nine months later—"

"My parents adopted her and loved her as their own. They never guessed it might have been you."

He did something that took her breath away. He pulled her into his arms and kissed her cheek, then just held her. "I'm sorry, Sarah. I would never have thought I'd have done what I did."

"I'm a preacher's kid, too, you know. And I got pregnant."

He released her and took her hand again. Together they strolled around the side of the house into the backyard, listening to the shuf-shuf-shuffing of their footsteps through the freshly mown lawn. She glanced over her shoulder toward the sliding glass doors that led to the back patio, and she hesitated. There stood Emma, her expression one of childlike delight. She nodded and smiled and mouthed the words, "Go, sis!"

Sarah tugged on Nick's hand and nodded toward the window. Together they waved.

"Our child." Nick caught his breath. "She doesn't know?"

Sarah shook her head. "She's never seen me as anything but her loving, overly protective sister."

"Is she the reason you never married?" he asked.

She sighed. The whole truth was going to be a little more difficult to expose. "She's my life. I had to be forced out of the family home by my parents, who wanted me to live a 'normal' life, whatever they meant by that."

"How could they expect that?"

She looked up at him and wanted to wrap her arms around him and kiss him and never let go. He understood.

"Thank you," she said. "Finally, someone who—"

"Knows what you're thinking? Didn't I always?"

Yeah, but she had to keep her wits about her. Mustn't get carried away. "Look, Nick, the only reason I told you and Edward about Emma was...well, to bring some joy back into your lives and make sure you knew the truth at last. You deserve that. But I'm not asking for anything from you. She's not your responsibility, and you have no legal obligations."

"But I want them. I'm her father, Sarah."

"Mom and Dad made her the beneficiary of a life insurance policy that will see her into adulthood, college, anything she needs."

"I'm not talking about that—though I want to do that, too. I'm talking about being her father. Teaching her. Loving her. Giving her what she lost when Mark...died."

"I know we'll be able to work things out as soon as we catch her attacker." But Sarah felt herself pulling away, both emotionally and physically. She released his hand and withdrew a couple of feet from his side. She wouldn't take advantage of Nick's natural desire to be a real father to his daughter. He could do that without marrying her mother.

She'd expected this part to hurt, but she hadn't been prepared for the depth of the pain.

He stopped walking and frowned at her. "Sarah? What's wrong?"

"This is an emotional time for both of us. We can't get caught up in all of it and lose sight of what we're dealing with."

"We'll keep her safe. Don't worry."

"I know that. What I'm saying is that we're different people now." He'd moved on with his life. She hadn't.

"I'm sure with a little more practice we'll be able to finish one another's sentences again."

"I think we're already doing that."

"Here's the thing, Sarah," he said when they reached the shrubs that bordered the lawn in the back of the property. "If we had known sixteen years ago what we know today, I would have married you."

"But that isn't how it worked out." She'd refused to impose herself into his life then, and she wouldn't do it now. Wouldn't take advantage of his good heart. The only thing worse than not having Nick would be having him in her life when she didn't know for sure he wanted to be there.

"And yet now you're here, I'm here and Emma believes she's an orphan, but she has a grandfather, a father and a mother on this very property right now. All three of us are crazy about her, and you obviously need help keeping up with her, if the past twenty-four hours are any indication."

Sarah found herself mesmerized by those dark eyes. This moment was like one of her teen dreams, the two of them grown up, still together, loving each other...

That was the problem. Loving each other? They didn't even know each other anymore.

"Stay here with us, Sarah."

"I've already agreed to stay a few days."

He pulled her to him again. She wanted to relax and melt into those arms, but she couldn't. As he'd said, if he'd known sixteen years ago what he knew now, he would have married her, and she'd have gone along with it because it would have been right. She was still, in reality, an unwed mother. She had her hands full with Emma, and her parents weren't around to help her. Nick was exactly the kind of man who would do the right thing and marry the mother of his child.

She would never forget this moment. In one way, it was a dream come true. The scent of grass and hay from the field behind them, the smell of clean sweat from Nick's skin, the sound of a tractor somewhere in the distance and the fishy odor of Capps Creek, the warm May air on her skin… But this dream wouldn't last. After all these years, she still believed in love—reality love, not just an act of doing the right thing.

"Give Emma a chance to get to know her father and grandfather," Nick said. "We'll catch the killer, and even if we don't, if someone wants to get to Emma, that person can get her across the state as easily as here."

Sarah hadn't considered any of this; what if they spent a summer in Jolly Mill getting to know one another better, and because of the gentleman he was, Nick asked her to marry him despite a lack of true love? He didn't know her anymore. The only thing worse than never having Nick in her life was having him there when she didn't know for sure he wanted to be.

"Will you stay?" Nick asked again.

It would be the hardest thing in the world to turn Nick away, but she refused to use Emma to lure him into a trap.

"We'll get him," Nick said. "We'll get the killer."

"But until then—"

"Until then we'll keep you and Emma as safe as if you were my own family. Because you are."

"I can only deal with one life-changing situation

at a time. If Emma and I stayed for the summer, I know how hard it would be for you to let her go."

"Then don't leave," he said softly.

"First things first," she said. "I want to make sure no killer gets to Emma."

"What about after we catch him?" He caressed her cheek, leaning so close she thought he might try to kiss her.

"As I said, first things first." She forced herself to turn around and walk away. It was one of the hardest things she'd ever done.

TWELVE

Nick was seated comfortably between his chattering daughter and her serene mother and staring into the soulful, love-filled eyes of Nina, who hadn't left Emma's side since being introduced to her. The Doberman had even followed Emma to the bathroom and waited outside until her new best friend came out. According to Edward, Carmen had bragged for months that she had the smartest dog on the planet. Tonight Nick believed it.

Sarah's nearness, the grassy-floral scent of her perfume—or maybe that was from the shampoo she'd just used when bathing in the guest suite— intoxicated him. He was exactly where he wanted to be, and he'd never expected to experience such overwhelming joy combined with such a bittersweet ache. Sarah was withdrawing.

And now the very child to whom he'd been introduced last night was in harm's way. But he couldn't imagine a place where she would be more protected than here in Carmen's fortified home with an attack dog trying to crawl up into Emma's lap for a cuddle—she'd done it once already—and with alarms at every door. And with men from the town circling the house.

Across from the sofa where Nick enjoyed the company of two beautiful young women, he faced Dad and Carmen, who sat together on a pretty yellow love seat. Carmen and Emma chattered nonstop, sharing, as they did, the same gregarious gene.

Was there a single person in this room besides Emma who couldn't see the way her eyes and her chin matched Dad's? Carmen had recently decorated using a picture on the wall of herself and several friends, including Mom, teasing and acting goofy for the camera. Had Emma not studied that picture closely? Or the photos of Nick with Mom and Dad on their own walls at home?

Of course, why would she be looking for similarities? She'd been raised to believe she was a Russell daughter.

Lynley Marshal—an old classmate of Nick's and Sarah's—sat with her mother, Kirstie, at the kitchen table with Nora, the three of them talking softly among themselves. Every so often they glanced toward Emma. Every so often, Carmen would catch Nick's gaze and wink, then nod toward Sarah.

Obviously, Carmen had somehow guessed.

He caught his father's gaze when he could distract him long enough from Emma. Dad smiled, nodded, and the smile remained, grew tender, as his attention once again shifted to his granddaughter.

A flash of light swept across the front windows, and Emma stiffened next to Nick.

"Don't worry. Alec's outside with Chapman," Nick said.

Emma nodded. "Edward's fishing buddy."

"Yep. He owns a lot of the land around here, and he's got a couple of cousins with him. I'm getting ready to take my shift in a few—"

Headlights swung into the driveway and the quiet purr of an engine died. All grew silent for a moment.

Sarah stood up. "I recognize that sound. John's here. Finally."

Nick stood with her. "We'd better get out there and warn everyone before he gets attacked by friendly fire."

She rushed to the front door, then into the arms of a man as tall as Nick, with short, auburn hair and a relieved smile. Nick suppressed a surprising twinge of jealousy. Cousins. They were cousins. John Fred Russell, the police officer from Sikeston, wore old tennis shoes, cut-off denims and a ragged T-shirt that didn't conceal the breadth of his shoulders or his movie-star looks. No wonder Emma wanted him to meet Lynley Marshal. Every woman in this room would want him to meet Lynley.

"Did you bring the albums?" Sarah asked her cousin as she released him and ushered him inside.

"In the car. Wanted to see Emma and whup the stuffing out of her first." He said it loudly enough for Emma to hear. Nick couldn't miss the affection in the man's eyes.

"Hey, you're not the police here." Emma jumped up, obviously too fast, and wobbled.

John rushed forward to catch her as Nick grabbed her from behind.

"I'm fine." She giggled. "But that proves you can't whup up on me. Nick says if I hit my head again I could die."

John sobered. He slowly released her and met Nick's gaze. "So this is Dr. Tyler." He held out a hand and Nick shook with him while they sized one another up in gentlemanly fashion. John nodded, as if satisfied, and glanced at Emma with a smile.

No missing the meaning in that expression. Officer John Russell, Sarah's cousin and confidante, knew everything. Nick could only hope Sarah had warned him not to tell Emma yet.

Emma took control of her cousin and introduced him to Dad and Carmen. Without a word being said, Nora, Kirstie and Lynley joined the group in the living room and surrounded John like a pack of hungry—

No. They were simply showing their southern Missouri hospitality. Watching from the sidelines, Nick was struck by a shock wave of memories as old friends met new. John had a heavier accent than the others—he could have been born and raised in the Deep South—but he had a serious, kind demeanor, and didn't seem to notice that everyone in the house was urging Lynley toward him until Nora blatantly explained that Lynley had just earned her doctorate in nursing and had been so busy she hadn't had time to get married. And then Emma explained, just as blatantly, that John's beloved wife had passed away six years ago in a drunk driving accident, which was what made him decide to become a policeman.

Then, of course, Carmen and Kirstie moved in for the kill—John didn't know they already had him married with children in their minds—and Nick couldn't resist a smile. Old habits. Some things never changed. He took comfort in that and thought about Alec's request for him to consider working at the clinic. What if he did? Sure, he loved the serenity of lawn care, but a guy couldn't just blow off a dozen years of hard work and study to risk melanoma and mow lawns for a living. Besides, when he was in a healthy frame of mind—unlike the past couple of years—he loved working with patients.

He'd always known he would return to the medical field, but not in the city, and not on an assembly line of patients. He wasn't a greedy man, didn't want to become wealthy. He just wanted a quiet life, time to treat patients thoroughly and a family to come home to at night.

He glanced at Sarah, who stood watching their

daughter with such unreserved love in her eyes that he imagined he felt a hard thump in the region of his chest.

But he couldn't act on impulse. They needed time. Lots of time. After sixteen years of zero direct communication—except for the constant reminders about her from his parents—one day of reacquainting himself with her was enough for him to know he wanted to be in her life again, but what he wanted and what would happen could be completely different.

Sarah stepped over to him and took his arm. "Come with me. I want to show you and Edward and Carmen…" She glanced toward Emma, then leaned up and whispered into his ear. "And everyone else what you should have been able to share with us for the past sixteen years." She looked over at John, who was surrounded by admirers. "Hey, cuz," she called. "Your car door unlocked?"

John nodded and waved her away as Nora, Kirstie and Carmen all tried to talk to him at once, and Lynley, for once, stood far from the middle of the group, shyly observing.

With a chuckle, Sarah led Nick outside where Alec stood watch. Gerard pulled up, parked in front of the house and got out.

"Any news from the Collinses?" Nick asked Gerard.

"Just spoke with the judge. His wife was afraid to

tell me earlier, but Cindy told Chaz she discovered holes poked in the gas line that fed into the building. He was doing some follow-up after the second explosion when he started getting calls. That was when he stopped telling his mother anything. The sheriff couldn't get anything out of him, and neither could the rural fire chief, but when Mrs. Collins took it upon herself to go looking for the pipes leading into the conference center, they'd been removed. I checked for myself, and any footprints had been wiped clean in the cellar."

"What about the scent?" Nick asked. "Did you catch anything like that?"

"I did indeed." Gerard leaned his elbow against John's red Chevy sedan. "I take it your cousin got here, Sarah?"

"He's inside being married off to Lynley as we speak," Sarah said. "What scent?"

"Cinnamon, as we'd suspected, but that wasn't all. Seems the building was constructed over a sinkhole. Some of the boards were loose, and I caught a strong scent of cooking smells, so I lifted a few of the boards. Doesn't appear that I was the only one doing that recently."

Sarah tapped Nick's arm. "The cave."

Nick nodded. "I'd forgotten."

"What're you two talking about?" Alec inched closer to them.

"Remember when we got into trouble for exploring the cave?" Sarah asked.

"You and Nick were always climbing around down there until you found some old skeletons that some forensics guy dated back to about the mid-eighteen-hundreds."

"You're kidding me," Gerard said. "You two made history?"

"Just discovered it," Sarah said. "The cavern had some dangerous drops, so the powers that be had concreted the main entrance—"

"Those powers being Chapman and my mother," Alec said.

Sarah shrugged. "So we found another way in."

"Why am I not surprised?" Gerard chuckled. "You two seemed to be something of a legend in these parts."

"We found one passage that led down beneath the creek," Nick said. "It was wet going, but we found a grate over the basement of my uncle's restaurant."

"That was the day we got caught," Sarah said. "Nick pushed the grate out, and his uncle Will just happened to be working down there. We never followed the passage to the other end. What if it comes out in the conference room cellar?"

"I didn't follow the cavern far," Gerard said, "but it looks well-used. You might want to ask your cousin about it."

Nick nodded to Alec. "What do you think?"

"He and his crew catered that retreat, didn't they? That would've placed him in the right place at the right time."

"I'm not talking about what you want to believe." There was a suspicious edge to Gerard's voice.

Nick felt a tightening in his stomach.

Alec scowled at Gerard. "I'm surprised you haven't dug into my past."

"Who says I haven't? I found a man who wouldn't risk his family businesses for restitution against a small-town church pastor he believed failed him."

"Oh, he failed my mother and me, all right, and she suffered dearly for it."

Sarah gasped as if she'd been punched in the stomach. Nick's arm circled her shoulders, and she leaned into the comfort they offered.

"Alec," Nick said, "I don't believe Nora would have raised you to speak ill of the dead, especially now, in front of Mark's daughter."

Alec rubbed his eyes, head bowed. "Sarah, I'm sorry. I didn't mean—"

"I remember you quit attending church a few months before we moved to St. Louis," she said. "Nora was obviously upset about it, but neither of you ever said why."

"Mom didn't know why. Your father did, though." The barest thread of sadness filtered through Alec's voice. "Now she'll always be a suspect in the eyes of the town." He looked at Gerard. "Thanks to you."

"I didn't reveal your family secrets," Gerard said. "And I don't think the town discovered anything new about Nora that they didn't already know. She's a strong woman who will fight to the death for her own life or the life of a friend."

Alec shook his head. "You wanted what you wanted, and that was the rehab center on the hill. You got it. My mother paid the price."

Nick's arms tightened more firmly around Sarah's shoulders. "You two are getting off the subject. Alec, you're still angry with Gerard because he outsmarted Nora when she tried to block the zoning change for his rehab center. We all know you wouldn't have killed his nurse to get even."

"You know me better than that."

Sarah gently shrugged from Nick's embrace. "Is someone going to tell me what you're talking about?"

Alec closed his eyes and shook his head, then turned his back to everyone. "I saw my father shoving my mother during one of his drinking sprees. I'd seen bruises on her arms before, and once, when I accidentally walked in on her dressing, there was a bruise on her back. I did what any Christian kid my age would do—I went to my pastor for help." He spat the words as if he'd tasted poison.

Sarah swallowed. She knew there'd been times in her father's life when church members seemed to think of him as God Himself. But Mark Russell was just a man who did the best he could and tried hard to help as many as possible. "He wasn't able to help you?"

"Oh, he tried." Alec's voice broke. "He spoke to my father, tried to run interference, and got a black eye for his trouble. My father? He just got meaner. That's when I lost faith in Mark Russell, and I thought I lost faith in God. I never had a chance to reconcile with Mark." He looked back at Sarah. "I'll always be sorry about that. My mother and I were both devastated by the deaths."

"What about God?" Sarah asked. "Have you reconciled with Him?"

"We're working on it, okay?"

"Well, you're off the hook with me, anyway," Gerard said. "A man newly in love isn't likely to go around hurting people in a grudge match."

"But the Russells and the Tylers were loved in town," Alec said. "I don't know of a soul around here who would've held a grudge against them."

His words seemed to echo what others believed. But they were all missing something.

"You know what?" Alec said. "No one's going to try anything tonight with so many others here. I think I'll head out and surprise my girl." He chuckled, but it sounded forced to Sarah. "She tends to be the jealous type, and the thought of me hanging around here with all these beautiful females is about to drive her nuts. I'll check back in later."

Gerard watched Alec walk away, then frowned at Nick. "I think I'll take a walk around the perimeter. Hey, Alec, wait up." Gerard fell into step as Alec strolled toward his car, which was parked at the back of the house.

Sarah opened the back door of John's sedan and found a full box of albums and photos her parents had taken of Emma over the years. "Emma won't be interested in looking at these for the thousandth time," she said.

"If she's a typical teenager, she'll be embarrassed," Nick said. "But I can't wait to get my hands on them."

"Good. Everyone else in the house would love to see these." She paused, glanced at him, pulled open one of the album covers. "Her junior prom photo."

He grinned. "As beautiful as her mother. The only two things I want more than to delve into these pictures is to protect this child—which means I'll stay out here for a while with Gerard—and before he finishes his rounds, I want to do this." He reached up. Cupping her chin with his hand, he lowered his lips to hers. She caught her breath and then allowed herself to drift with the moment.

His lips were firm, reassuring, filling her with so much joy she didn't want to contain it. His touch gave her courage she hadn't realized she had, and she felt safe.

When he released her, she stared through the darkness into his eyes, questioning.

"Do you remember our first kiss sixteen years ago?" he asked.

She shook her head.

"Neither do I. Not well, anyway." He sighed and drew her against him, his arms strong and protective—the way she knew they would protect their daughter. She hesitated, then allowed herself to rest her cheek against his shoulder.

"For so long I wondered why God allowed your father to take you away from Jolly Mill," he said.

"I think Alec gave us an inkling about that. I believe Dad knew he'd mismanaged the situation with Nora and Eaton Thompson, and he hated that Alec left the church."

"Your father was an excellent minister. Dad always said so. He was young and inexperienced. I'm sure he developed all the experience he needed."

"Our church in Sikeston thought so."

"Mark Russell left a church of hurting members behind, and they've never been satisfied with anyone since he went away."

"Dad wouldn't have been happy about that."

"I understand from our daughter that he also wasn't happy that you never dated much, and you could have had your pick."

"Wasn't interested in picking."

"That's what I heard. Emma's words, not mine. But really? Sarah, you're so beautiful."

She felt a flush travel up her face. "Skin deep doesn't mean much."

"I'm not talking about skin. I'm talking about your heart, your loyalty. You couldn't leave Emma."

She allowed his words to flow over her. It was nice to know he appreciated her maternal instincts, but that wasn't enough.

"And now Emma has a biological father and grandfather she has yet to get to know," she said.

Nick took Sarah's bare, ringless hand and caressed it, making her breath skitter from her lungs. "She also has a wonderful mother who loves her more than life itself."

Her heart took a few seconds between beats. "It nearly killed me to give her to them for adoption, even though I got to name her and stay near her. I fed her naturally and spent as much time as possible with her."

Despite all that, she'd ached with the knowledge that Emma wasn't hers in the eyes of the world.

"I desperately need time to get to know my flesh and blood," Nick said. "I want to give Dad time to get to know her. You didn't see him before Emma arrived last night, and I saw his face when he saw you for the first time this morning. Having you and

Emma here has made all the difference in the world, not just for Dad, but for me. I'm being totally selfish."

"Of course. I understand." She did understand. How painful this could be.

"And why should you and Emma rattle around together, just the two of you, in that house in Sikeston, when you could be surrounded by old friends and family here for the summer? It would give us all time to heal together."

He'd already convinced her Emma would be safer here than in Sikeston with a killer still on the loose. But afterward?

"All she's ever known were Mom and Dad," Sarah said. "The truth is going to be such a shock. I can only imagine what that could do to her."

"But you'll have to tell her."

"I will, of course, but maybe I should choose the time carefully."

"Don't you think she's going to find out very quickly what everyone else is already guessing?"

"Yes, and I can't help thinking her heart will be broken when she discovers those wonderful people she loved as her parents weren't actually her parents."

"That heart can heal."

"Not as easily as people expect."

"I know there's an old adage about never being able to return home again, but are you brave enough to try?"

"I'm here now, aren't I?" In sixteen years, Sarah realized she'd never stopped looking for Nick in the eyes of other men. If she spent the summer here, close to him, seeing him every day, or at least several times a week, wouldn't she suffer heartbreak all over again when the summer ended and she had to return to Sikeston? She didn't want Nick to make some noble gesture simply because he believed marrying his daughter's mother was the right thing to do.

If she'd learned anything since the night she became pregnant, it was that no matter that he'd held her, if it wasn't her he believed he was kissing and holding, it meant nothing.

Nick pulled her close again, and despite all her inner fear and resistance, she relished the feel of his arms around her and the sound of his voice so close to her ear. Had that been her response the night of the party, as well?

He placed his hand at the back of her head and kissed her cheek. She closed her eyes and resisted the urge to turn her head and meet that kiss full on.

"You obeyed your parents. You honored them. You gave up the child you obviously love for unselfish reasons—because you believed your parents could give her the solid foundation she needed."

"I've often wondered if I was simply afraid of the responsibility."

"Not you. I never saw you back down from anything."

She raised the box of photos. "I know Edward and Carmen will want to see these. As soon as you can come back in, you'll see them, too."

He pulled a high school photo from the loose ones and studied it in the low light. "Alec was right. She really does look like Mom did at that age. I'm still in awe of Emma."

"She's her own person."

"Like you were, only without the black goop."

Sarah chuckled. "Actually, she takes after her aunt Shelby."

Nick took Sarah's hand and kissed it. "Emma needs her parents, and that's us."

A movement of brush reached them from the shadows, and Sarah gasped.

Gerard's hulking shadow rounded John's car. "A guy can learn a lot if he treads lightly."

Nick groaned aloud. "Everyone on the planet's going to know we're Emma's parents before we have a chance to tell her."

"Believe me," Gerard said, "there's nothing I'd love more than to hear this story, but Megan just alerted me on my earphone that she saw someone running across the road from the direction of the clinic, then disappear in the hedges. Nick, if you'll stay put for a minute I think I'll put Sarah's cousin to work." With casual movements he climbed the porch steps toward the front door. He didn't appear alarmed, and his calm demeanor kept Sarah from panicking. Still, she followed him, and her heart rate had increased a couple of miles an hour.

THIRTEEN

Nick was stepping onto the porch behind Sarah when John came rushing out of the house, looking grim as he strapped on a chest holster and slid a weapon into its slot.

"Get into the house, cuz. Nick, you got a weapon?"

"I brought Dad's extra .380, but—"

"That'll do," John said. "Sarah Fey, you never did listen well. I'm serious. Get into the house *now.* Alec got another call from Gerard's wife, Megan. She's been watching over the town from the hillside through this really cool night-vision telescope gadget. Wish I had one. Anyway, she caught the outline of someone leaving Parker's Diner and coming on foot in this direction, keeping to the shadows."

"But that's the opposite direction of the clinic, where the Chapmans saw their culprit," Nick said.

John shrugged. "We're being proactive here, okay? Could be anyone. It's not as if we've got killers all over town, but it won't hurt to check everything out. Megan's pretty sure the figure she saw coming from the diner wasn't big enough to be Billy Parker, and the diner closed over an hour ago."

"Well, sure, but sometimes it takes over an hour to clean and prep for the next day," Sarah said.

Nick considered Petra Journigan, but Alec had left to see her a few moments ago. Right? "Any idea who it might have been?"

"She couldn't make out much, and whoever it was wore all black clothing and a stocking cap."

Nick nudged Sarah toward into the house away from the open front door. "Stay inside for now, please?"

"Okay, but this house is already being guarded like Fort Knox. Do you mind not hitting the streets in search of trouble? Emma's the one we need to protect, and she's right here. Ever heard of a red herring? What if those two people are just distractions—one friend going over to another friend's house to watch TV? If you men take off looking for trouble, who's going to be around if trouble comes here from another direction?"

Dad stepped through the door, nodding. "This girl always did make sense." He sounded perfectly relaxed. "Besides, she's an author in her spare time, and she knows all about red herrings."

"I thought you wanted to show everyone pictures of Emma," Nick said. "Now's a good time for that."

Sarah continued to hesitate. The woman always

did have that stubborn streak. Now was not the time for it.

"Sarah, now. Remember what I told you," he said. "First, I'm seeing to her safety. There's a psychopath who isn't afraid to kill to protect himself." He reached for the door, still holding her gaze.

"Relax, Sarah," Gerard called through the door to her. "Nick's hit more bull's-eyes than I have."

Nick caught Sarah's pointed look. "Okay, I have to admit, Sarah, you used to outshoot me in high school, but I've had practice since then. Turn on the alarms and stay in the house."

He couldn't bear the fear he saw in her eyes. "Make sure Emma's aware she's still in danger."

Sarah nodded. "Be careful." She pressed her hand against the window. "Please, please be careful."

"Don't worry, I'll stay behind Gerard. He's the biggest shield in town."

Gerard grunted. "If I didn't need you for backup I'd—"

"Yeah, but you've been out of the business for a while." Nick waited until he heard the door latch click. He turned back to Gerard and walked down the steps beside him.

"The kid looks like you," Gerard said.

"Please never tell her that," Nick said. "No pretty young woman wants to be told she looks like her father."

"I just found out today." Dad strolled across the

lawn beside Gerard. "You know that high-speed chase we had? That was my reaction."

"You had a high-speed chase and I missed it?" John complained. "I knew I should've come with Sarah last night."

"Have you tried to reach the sheriff again?" Nick asked.

"And tell him what? Someone's walking around town and we think they might be killers? Most of the deputies are tied up with a meth lab bust down south of Neosho. It would take someone at least forty-five minutes to reach us."

"So we're on our own," Nick said. "Where did Alec really go when he left here?"

"He said he was going to see his girl."

"Oh, that's right, his excuse was a jealous girl-friend." Nick couldn't keep the sarcasm from his voice. "Since when did Alec Thompson let a neurotic female keep him on a leash?"

"That's what I asked him when I walked him to his car." Gerard chuckled. "My opinion wasn't appreciated."

Nick glanced over at him in the light from the porch. "You still don't trust him."

"I'm not sure what to think, but not all the facts are in yet. I checked the tires and bumper of his car earlier, and there was no evidence that he could have rammed poor Chaz into the river."

"I don't suppose you checked Nora's automobiles? She has an old farm truck in the barn she seldom uses."

Gerard nodded. "Granted, I've had my run-ins with Alec, but he's not the kind of man to drag his mama into his fights, or use her automobiles to kill someone. I checked anyway. All clean. I have an idea Alec suspects something he's not telling us, and I've seen Nora watching him strangely from time to time today—after all, a mother knows her child."

"Maybe someone should ask Nora." Nick looked at Dad.

"I could have a talk with her," Dad said. "But if she suspects Alec's involved, you know how she'll be. Like a mama tiger."

"But she's always had a soft spot for you, hasn't she?" Gerard asked.

"She and Peg were good friends, and Nora's brought her fair share of meals by since…" He swallowed.

"Dad, you and John need to keep watch from here," Nick said.

"Stay in the shadows," Gerard said. "Nick, coming with me?"

"You can be sure John's not getting far from his baby cousin. Besides, it could be a false alarm. We don't have any idea who we're looking for, do we?"

"Someone dressed in black."

"I knew I should've worn my uniform," John muttered. "Why doesn't this town have a police force?"

"Don't usually need 'em," Dad said.

"But when we need them, we need more than one," Gerard said. "Guess that's why the good Lord brought you across the state, Officer Russell. You know, this town could always use another ex-cop for support at times like this."

"Tempting offer," John muttered as he fell back. "But I'm not an ex-cop, I'm about to become a detective."

Nick continued walking with Gerard. "Have you considered why Alec didn't loop us in on his plans tonight?"

"Do you go around telling everyone when you're going out on a date?"

"That was a flat-out lie and you know it."

"He and your cousin Billy used to be friends."

"You still suspect my cousin?" Nick asked.

"Mr. Parker Jr. might be related to you, but he's a hot-headed, coldhearted businessman. If he thinks there's still a chance you could inherit that diner out from under him…" Gerard shrugged. "Sarah's parents could have been collateral damage. After all, his father's still alive, so the way father and son seem to dislike each other, Billy might have been afraid his father might still want to give the diner to his sister."

"My cousin's a jerk, but he wouldn't have killed his

own flesh and blood." Nick felt uncomfortable even saying those words. How would he know what Billy would or would not do? They'd never gotten along.

"You've studied psychiatry?" Gerard asked.

"Not criminal psychology."

"You know this town. You need to help me figure out who has my wife stirred up enough to call about her suspect. She has a special sense about these things." Gerard nudged Nick into the darker shadows beneath the mature trees that lined the street. "Meanwhile we can check in at the diner and find out who just left there."

"Or intercept whoever's coming from there."

"Good idea." Gerard's voice dropped to a whisper as they continued down the street. He tapped his right ear, spoke softly, tapped it again. "Time to head west. Megan saw our shadow turn right into that copse of trees behind the general store."

"Carmen and Nora offered to take a turn keeping watch outside," Nick murmured softly.

"That's what Megan told me. She's keeping in contact with the house, as well," Gerard whispered. "Now hush."

Nick glanced over his shoulder. All seemed quiet. He couldn't see Dad or John, and he doubted they could see him or Gerard.

But the farther away from the house he and Gerard got, the less comfortable he felt. He didn't like leaving Sarah and his daughter there without him.

* * *

Sarah tucked her bare feet beneath her and placed two scrapbooks between herself and Carmen on the love seat. Nina seemed to have trouble deciding whether she loved Emma or Sarah the best, but since Emma was willing to roughhouse on the floor with her and give her special treats, her stomach issued the verdict.

Kirstie and Lynley Marshal had scooted their chairs closer to Nora to peruse the loose photos John had brought of the whole Russell family.

Carmen paged through the first scrapbook and giggled, pointing to one shot of Emma with long braided deep brown pigtails. "How old was she here?"

"Nine. She cut them off soon after, and Mom saved the hair."

"I think I have a picture just like this of me at that age," Carmen said. "And now I remember my real hair color."

"Dark brown?"

"With nice, wide streaks of white now, which is why I keep it blond." Carmen narrowed her eyes at Sarah. "You know, you look somewhat like a turkey two days before Thanksgiving."

Sarah ran her fingers through her hair. "I took a shower, I used your shampoo, and if I must say so myself, your hair dryer did a great job with the layers, so I don't know what you mean."

Carmen gave her a toothy grin and binked her on the nose with a forefinger. "Your eyes give you away. Look, we've got all the curtains and blinds pulled shut, and, honey, believe me, I'm a crack shot."

"I'm better," called black-haired, exotic Nora from the table.

"Only because you have a better revolver."

"And why is that?" Nora asked.

"Because you have the wisdom to purchase the best," chorused Kirstie, Lynley and Carmen together.

Carmen placed a hand on Sarah's shoulder. "Honey. We have three doors on this level, none upstairs, only one basement entrance, and the men can see them all from where they're posted."

"Even though the poor fellas don't realize it's not necessary to surround the house," Kirstie said, "we'll let them think they're big, strong men, and we poor, helpless ladies couldn't do without their help."

Nora grunted. "I've done without a man around the house for as long as your sweet Emma's been alive, and believe me, it can be a lot of fun."

Kirstie muttered, "Here we go again."

While the women continued to chatter and badger one another in the dining room, Carmen leaned over and whispered in Sarah's ear. "Guess you heard about Nora's husband."

Sarah nodded.

"Hey, kiddo," Nora called. "You gossiping about me in there?"

"Sure am," Carmen drawled. "What're you gonna do about it?"

"You know those cinnamon biscotti I make for your birthday every year?"

"Nonsense. I no longer have birthdays. I'm forty-nine and holding."

"Oh, pshaw," Kirstie snorted, and then her daughter got tickled and giggled. "You can't hold on to your age."

"I plan to."

"Anyway," Nora said with raised voice, "since you'll no longer have birthdays, those yummy biscotti won't be in your birthday basket when the date comes around again."

"Not fair!"

"Ha! And tell me how you'll convince that gorgeous Edward Tyler five years from now that you're still forty-nine?"

Carmen shot Sarah a sheepish look. "I'm not trying to trick Edward Tyler into anything, Nora. A man who appreciates a woman for her inner beauty is the best kind of man of all."

"So!" Kirstie said. "You did date Edward, after all."

"He robbed the cradle. He was a senior when I hit high school." Carmen glanced at Sarah. "It's nice to have a small school so we younger girls had more opportunities with the upperclassmen."

"And you were heartbroken when he started dating Peg."

Carmen hesitated. "For about two days, then I developed a crush on—"

"Yeah, we know. You liked older guys," Nora said. "I'm surprised you ever settled down long enough to get married."

"And widowed," Carmen reminded her.

Silence reigned for a few seconds.

"And then there was Nick and Sarah," Kirstie said. "Madly in love for years."

"We were the best of friends," Sarah said, casting a quick look toward Emma, who seemed not to be listening.

"Well," Nora said, "I still think Carmen cares about Edward. Oh, not the heart-racing, breathless love of youth—may we never be cursed with that hideous experience again—but her affection is more mature, almost manageable, and I wouldn't mind at all if Carmen and Edward would one day—years from now—become friends again."

"I don't suppose you'll give Edward a choice?" Sarah asked the ladies.

"Oh, fiddlesticks," Nora said. "Everyone knows a man needs a woman more than a woman needs a man."

"Who said that?" Carmen asked.

"Me. Just now. Get a good one, and you'll feel like a queen. Get a rotten one, and your life is over."

"Aha!" Carmen said. "I just happened to remember something. Maybe Alec really did have a good reason to rush away and find Petra. Did you know that when she arrived here with her family her sophomore year, Nick was nice to her, and she immediately developed a crush on him?"

"I do remember that," Sarah said. She also remembered what jealousy felt like, even though she knew Nick was simply being kind to the new girl.

"In fact," Carmen said, "remember our little party that didn't turn out so well?"

"The drugs," Nora grumbled. "I wouldn't have been surprised if the D.A. had attempted to add that into the mix in court this past year, as well."

"Oh, hush," Lynley said. "You know we'd have never let him do that."

"Poor Petra kept looking for Nick at the party that night," Carmen said. "I wasn't about to break her heart and tell her I'd seen him with Shelby. I mean, I was surprised enough, myself, to see him with the wrong twin. One never saw Nick without Sarah."

Sarah cleared her throat and glanced at Carmen. "Well, about that. Um…well, you see, Shelby was sick that night, and I decided to wash off all that goop."

Carmen gasped. "That was you with Nick I saw kissing up in the loft?"

The room fell silent and all the women stared at Sarah. Emma continued playing with Nina, but Sarah knew that hyper-vigilant expression on her daughter's face.

"You know what else?" Carmen piped up. "If you want to talk about love tangles, guess who was looking for Petra that same night."

Sarah was afraid to ask. She glanced at the others.

"Nick's cousin," Carmen said.

Kirstie gasped. "Billy? Carmen, why didn't you say anything?"

"Hello? Worse problems to deal with? Drugged soda? But I do recall the look of heartbreak on Billy's face when he was standing not too far from the table and Petra asked about Nick."

Nora suddenly stood up. "Okay, that does it. I'll never eat at Parker's again. Do you realize he might well have been the one to drug the soda? Remember the crowd he ran with then? Will Parker was always clamping down on his son. That Billy was a wild one. Who knows what he could put in our food any time he wants and no one would guess."

"Oh, sit down and look at more of these pictures." Kirstie tugged on Nora's sleeve, and Nora reluctantly gave in. The chatter grew once again.

Carmen touched Sarah's hand and held up one of the scrapbooks. Sarah caught her breath. It was a page with her photo, Aunt Peg's, Emma's and Mom's, all at the same age.

"You were the one with Nick the night Billy, or whoever, placed the drug in the sodas?"

Sarah nodded.

"Your parents adopted their granddaughter," she whispered.

"Yes."

Carmen leaned forward and beckoned Sarah to do the same. "She's yours," she said with such a beautiful thread of joy in her voice that it brought tears to Sarah's eyes. "Yours and Nick's?"

Sarah cast a warning glance toward Emma. "She doesn't know."

"Oh, honey, why didn't I see it sooner? We all should have. Good can come out of just about anything, can't it?"

"I'm still working on that. Emma's a really good thing, I know."

Carmen stretched out and rested her stockinged feet on the coffee table. She'd changed into her pajamas, and her lovely legs were partially exposed by the slit up the side of her pajama bottoms. She still carried the grace of her earlier years. She glanced toward Emma, snuggled beside Nina in the cozy sunroom. "She's a beautiful girl."

Sarah leaned her head into the sofa back, feeling the comfort of Carmen's encouraging words. It was true that she felt safer here, with family and old friends, than she would have felt driving back across the state. Also, she'd forgotten how much like Mom Carmen was.

"Thank you," she said softly.

"I'm just glad you're here," Carmen said. She nodded toward Emma. "That child sure came as quite a surprise for all of us when we heard about her, nine months after your family moved away. None of us could believe your mama would keep such a secret from us."

"It was a difficult situation." Sarah made sure the chatter of the others covered her voice.

"And they handled it with the typical Russell grace. I'm glad to see you and Nick together again after so many years," Carmen said. "You two were always good with each other."

"He was a good friend. He and Edward want us to stay for the summer."

Carmen glanced toward Emma. "So they know."

"I told them today."

"Aha! Let me guess—Nick wants to marry you."

"He can't want to marry me, Carmen. He doesn't even know me anymore, and when we were kids, he never showed that kind of interest in me."

"Of course not. He was bound for med school, and everyone knows marriages are difficult enough without that kind of hardship binding them down."

"It didn't stop him from marrying someone else. Besides, I'm a grown woman, not a helpless teenager. He just wants to get to know his daughter."

Carmen leaned next to Sarah's ear. "You telling her tonight?"

Sarah gazed down at her daughter and shook her head. "She's already endured so much."

Carmen patted Sarah's arm. "It might be difficult, but she'll come around."

"It was different for Edward and Nick. You wouldn't believe how happy they are about her."

"I'll be saying little prayers from now until you tell her."

"Thank you. Would you do me another favor?" Sarah asked. "Would you tell me about Nick? I've only heard snatches of information about him over the years when our parents spoke or met on retreats."

"Well, rest assured he realized his mistake with the marriage." Carmen aimed a pretty sneer toward the ceiling. "It might interest you to know that Dr. Nicolas Tyler was married for a total of five miserable years to 'Queen' Chloe, and I do mean miserable. Why he didn't look you up if he wanted to get married, I'll never know."

"It's because he didn't feel that way about me. Best friends, yes. Nothing more." The truth sank in more deeply.

"Then he was an idiot. Getting trapped by that gold digger who always wanted the most expensive car, the latest fashions, best jewelry, and of course she thought we Jolly Mill hicks were dirt under her feet. Not that I'm bitter."

Sarah forced a chuckle. "Of course not."

"I always did think you two were just right for each other, both of you being brainiacs and never interested in the outward markings of social vanity."

"Outward markings?" Sarah giggled. "You don't think my Goth getup was outward enough?"

"Oh, pshaw." Carmen shot her a dimpled grin. "That was rebellion, pure and simple. I have to say, I always admired you for your independence, even if you did embarrass your poor folks half to death the first day you pranced into church that way. And poor Shelby—she nearly fainted dead away in the pew. When Nora saw you, she snorted so hard the whole congregation was giggling by the time your dad stepped to the pulpit."

Sarah was just beginning to relax when Carmen's telephone screeched. Sarah jerked. Nina swung around from her playtime with Emma and barked, jumping up and down.

Carmen answered, listened, frowned. "Alec, honey, slow down." She got up and walked into the dining room where her friends sat watching her. Sarah followed.

"No, but Sarah's here." She held out the phone for Sarah. "Not sure what he's talking about, but I think you need to hear him."

Sarah took the phone. "Alec? What's up?"

"I just remembered something about Petra that I should've remembered a long time ago. Her last name changed after she moved here with her mother and stepfather."

"She had a different name?"

"Friedman."

Sarah gasped as she recognized that name. She'd heard it often after the Spring River retreat changed venue and poor Mr. Friedman took his own life.

"So you do recall the name," Alec said.

"Yes. Aren't you with her now? I thought you were going to see her tonight."

"I called her and she was working late on some new pastry experiment."

Sarah froze. "Something with cinnamon?"

"Hey, yeah, that's right. How'd you know? So I started thinking about my argument with Gerard. Mom wasn't the only one abused when I was growing up. I remembered the rumors about Petra, and so I had to check our old school yearbooks. Sure enough, I compared her former name to the name of the guy in Verona who committed suicide."

"Alec, where are you?"

"Home."

"I think the guys might need some help. Can you come back here? I've got to call Nick."

"But what—"

She disconnected, located Nick's cell number and punched it in, hoping he'd switched to vibrate. She didn't realize she'd been holding her breath until he answered.

"Yeah."

"Nick. It's Petra."

"What?"

"She was adopted by her stepfather, remember? Your hunch was correct. Her last name was Friedman before her stepfather adopted her. Alec checked our high school yearbook. I'd forgotten, but after we saw the bruises on her, we did some investigating and discovered the man was her stepfather. I was outraged when he had the audacity to adopt her and call himself her father."

There was a soft exhale.

"Edward tried to help her, remember? Couldn't that be why he received that call to get him out of the building?"

"It could. You're right. Sarah, stay indoors, but keep talking. It's going down any time."

"She must have been the source of the spicy scents Emma picked up today. She was working on a new pastry." She glanced toward Emma, who was suddenly paying too much attention, so she excused herself from the others and carried the phone into the guest bedroom.

"Petra helps with the catering for Parker's," she continued.

"Which makes sense, doesn't it?" Nick said. "She could have been at the conference center that day."

"Couldn't she have left an open chafing dish flame near those holes Chaz found punched into the gas pipe? What if Cindy saw her doing something to the gas line?"

"Keep talking. I'm with you." His voice was almost too soft to hear.

Sarah sank onto the bed. "Petra would have blamed Dad for her father's death. Who wouldn't be malleable at that age? She was looking for you at Nora's party. She had a crush on you and must've seen you and me together."

"It doesn't make sense that she'd want revenge over so innocent a thing all these years later."

"Except I'm Mark Russell's daughter. If she was at Parker's this morning when Emma came in, she could've heard Emma asking about the conference center. You know how Emma chatters with any stranger she meets. She'd have introduced herself and Petra couldn't have avoided the connection."

"You think she's still bent on revenge?" Nick asked.

"In her frame of mind, it wouldn't take much. How twisted could she have become after her father committed suicide—abandoning her in the most painful way—and then her stepfather beat her for who knows how long? We don't even know if she got help for that. If she's focused all her hatred toward Dad all these years, what's going to stop her from trying to wipe out his whole family? Even if she doesn't realize Emma's our daughter, Nick, she could have taken that underground passage to the cellar."

"Sounds as if we've found our psychopath."

"I teach kindergarteners, Nick. I don't know much about psychopathic killers." Sarah needed to go to Emma. It was time for the talk.

FOURTEEN

Blackness surrounded Nick with such persistence he nearly switched on his penlight against Gerard's orders, but he heard the creeping sound of footfalls approximately fifty yards away. Though the trees were thick in this patch of woods, he couldn't take the chance of the wrong person catching them.

"Something up?" Gerard asked in a soft whisper.

"Petra may be our killer."

"Alec tell you that?"

"Sarah."

More silence until Gerard tapped his earpiece and spoke into it. "Could we be looking for Petra?" he asked his wife, who was manning the phones and telescope.

Nick waited until something larger than a dog but smaller than a horse crept through the thickets of underbrush, coming their way.

"You think she was at the diner just thirty minutes ago?" he asked Megan, then gestured for Nick to slow down. "I think we're homing in on her. We'll have a little chat and get back to you, honey." He tapped his Bluetooth.

"What did Megan say?" Nick whispered.

"I'm guessing Petra has motive but her pining boss might be the reason Emma was born. And he has motive, as well."

"You're saying Billy could've killed my mother. His own aunt."

"I wouldn't put that past him, but I'm talking about the drugs. Your cousin was into the drug scene. Who better to have access to enough ecstasy to hype a bunch of kids at a party? And who would have gotten a better kick out seeing them mess up their lives?"

"So who's it going to be? Petra or Billy? Who would be happier to discover that you gave birth out of wedlock to Emma because of the effects of the drugs?"

Gerard tapped Nick on the shoulder. "Sounds as if one of them's coming this way. Let's wait for a few minutes."

Sarah stepped out of the guest room to find that everyone but Emma had clustered in the hallway.

"So it's Petra?" Nora asked.

"I'm not sure, but I've alerted Nick." Sarah glanced toward the living room. "Where's Emma?"

"She's in her room," Carmen said. "Nina's with her, of course, but, honey, something's up. She looked a little shocked, and she was right outside this door while you spoke with Nick. What did she hear?"

Sarah covered her mouth with her hand. No. She couldn't have heard. Could she?

"What did you and Alec talk about?" Carmen asked.

"I was talking to Nick, and I might have mentioned the fact that Emma's our daughter." *Breathe... have to breathe.* "I should have spoken with her sooner, but I wanted to wait until we found the killer. She's been through so much."

"Tell us, honey," Kirstie said.

"Petra was working with spices, like what Emma smelled, at the diner. She's also the daughter of the man who ran that Spring River retreat center. The one who killed himself when business dropped?"

"So she knew your dad was the one who moved the venue for the conferences." Carmen took Sarah in her arms. The others joined her until Sarah felt nearly suffocated by a human blanket.

"You want us to have a talk with her?" Nora asked. "You know how hurtful teenagers can be, and she'll hate herself later."

"She deserves to hear the truth from me."

"Want us to come with you, at least?" Kirstie asked. "Believe me, I've seen Lynley at her worst, and I'd have appreciated some protection at the time."

"Mom!" Lynley slapped her mother on the shoulder.

"See what I mean?"

"Come on, Sarah," Carmen said. "She likes us, I can tell. We can do a lot to lighten the mood."

"It's what we've done for one another for a lot of years," Nora said.

At one point tonight, Sarah had considered asking Nick to help her tell Emma the truth, but he was out in the night looking for a killer. This was her job.

"Just pray for me?" she asked.

"Oh, honey, you know we will." Carmen gave Sarah a final hug before she walked down the hallway to the closed door of Emma's guestroom.

"Emma, we need to talk," she said through the door.

All she heard was hard, heavy sniffling, heaving sobs.

Sarah opened the door and walked in. Nina whined and walked over to her, touched her wet nose to Sarah's hand, then walked back to Emma, who knelt beside her bed the way she used to as a child when she said her nighttime prayers.

Sarah knelt beside her and placed an arm around her shoulders. She expected Emma to stiffen or push her away, but she didn't move.

"I think now you know why I never wanted to leave home," she said. "I couldn't let you go. I love you the way a mother loves her child, and no matter what all the legal papers said, those papers didn't fit what was in my heart."

Emma cried harder.

Sarah sensed Carmen, Nora, Kirstie and Lynley hovering at the open doorway, and she felt the comfort of their presence.

Slowly, she told Emma about what happened the night of Nora's party, and how grateful she and Nick were that something good had come out of something intended for evil. She described the joy that Edward felt today, knowing Emma was his granddaughter, and how much Edward and Nick already loved her as their own. By the time she finished, Emma was no longer sobbing, but she also wasn't sitting up and hugging Sarah and telling her everything was okay.

"I need to be alone for a while," she said. "Can Nina stay with me?"

Leaving was the last thing Sarah wanted to do. "Of course. You want me to close the door?"

Emma nodded without looking up.

Feeling suddenly old and stiff, Sarah rose from her knees and turned to walk out of the room as tears once again made their familiar trails down her face.

"Hope my old handcuffs aren't too tight," Gerard said over the pathetic bursts of outrage from Petra Journigan, who continued to fight and scratch and kick as Nick helped Gerard herd her out of the forest and into Alec's waiting car.

"First of all, you can't arrest me for spiking soda

sixteen years ago." She tried again to jerk from Gerard's grasp. It didn't work. "Statute of limitations."

"Murder, however," Gerard said, "will have you in prison for life, and there's a deputy sheriff on his way here right now to pick you up."

She glared up at Gerard, then Nick, and spat on the ground. "That hypocritical pig, the almighty *Reverend* Mark Russell, was the reason my father died. The self-righteous faker killed my father's business. Daddy lived for that business!"

"And so you killed Reverend and Mrs. Russell and Mrs. Tyler—as well as my nurse, Cindy, and Chaz Cooper—to get back at one man?" Gerard asked.

She hunched forward. "You can't prove anything."

"So you're saying my old garden spade won't have your fingerprints on it from hitting Emma Russell in the head with it this morning? Her memory's coming back, you know."

The once-innocent-looking, scrubbed-clean face was fouled with bitterness. "You won't find my prints there."

"But we've already tracked your underground passage beneath Capps Creek," Nick said.

Petra stiffened.

"You didn't think we'd find that?" Nick resisted the urge to grab the woman and shake her—if he gave in, he might not stop. This person killed his mom. In fact, he shouldn't even be here.

"I didn't mean to… I wasn't after… Mark Russell was the only one who was supposed to get hurt, and I didn't use that passage this morning. Wasn't anywhere near it."

"Mark Russell never hurt anyone," Nick snapped. "He only wanted to protect people by moving the meetings away from tainted water. You took lives. You killed my mother, my friends—"

Gerard laid a hand on his arm and squeezed. Nick gritted his teeth and took a step backward.

"I don't know anything about Cindy or Chaz," Petra said.

"Nothing?" Gerard asked.

Petra's face crumpled. Tears dribbled from her eyes. She shook her head. "I never meant… Carol at the diner can tell you I was sleeping upstairs when that poor kid bought it. And I never drugged my classmates when we were in school, either."

Gerard shut Petra into the backseat of the car and looked at Nick. "You believe her?" he asked softly.

"I'm not in any condition to think about this rationally, but there's a back way out of the apartments upstairs. Carol couldn't have known if Petra was there."

"But don't you think it's strange she would admit to some of the killings, but not all?"

Nick held his friend's gaze. "You think we have more than one killer in Jolly Mill?"

"I don't think this night's over."

Nick glanced through the back window of the car

at Petra, hunched forward, trying to wipe her drippy nose on her sleeve with her hands cuffed behind her back. He felt sick to his stomach.

"I'll call Carmen's house and let them know about Petra, at least." Gerard glanced into the back of the car and sighed. "But I'm afraid she's not the only culprit."

Carmen disconnected her phone and turned to the others. "They caught the mad bomber!" she shrieked.

Sarah looked up from the pictures, stomach roiling.

Carmen stepped across the room and hugged her. "It was Petra. Oh, sweetheart, I'm so sorry. It seems she was the one who caused the explosion that killed your parents, but Gerard says we still need to stay inside and keep the alarms on."

"You mean they're not sure?"

"He doesn't think she did it all." Carmen turned and gestured toward the others. "Girls, why don't y'all wrap up some packages of Nora's latest dream cookies? We're going to owe our boys big-time for tonight's work."

"I wonder if Gerard would consider taking on a private job for Jolly Mill," Nora said. "With a growing population, our finances will increase, and we might as well make the most of it all. We could afford a policeman or two. It feels good to have protection close at hand."

Sarah rushed to tell Emma the news, but when she reached the room, the door stood open. Emma wasn't there. Nina stepped into the hallway, whining.

"Emma?" Sarah called at the bathroom door. There was no answer. She pushed the door open and it was empty. Nina whined again.

The latch on the front door clicked, and Sarah looked up just in time to see her daughter quickstepping down the sidewalk to the dark street.

"Oh, no you don't, young lady. Emma!"

But Emma had disappeared into the darkness at a run. She must have heard the first part of Carmen's announcement, deemed it safe to go outside and taken her chance before Sarah could warn her.

Nina pawed at the front door, and a growl rumbled in her throat.

Sarah looked over her shoulder. "Girls, Emma's out there, and I'm going after her." As soon as the door opened, Nina shoved her way through it and raced out into the darkness.

"Emma!" Sarah called into the night air. "Honey, come back inside. It's not safe out there yet!"

Sarah followed Nina, pressing Nick's cell number. She stumbled over a limb and wished she'd grabbed a flashlight.

Nick answered, and the sound of his voice brought her comfort, but not enough. "Nick, Emma just left the house before I could stop her. Nina's anxious about something. Where are you?"

"We're combing the woods between the creek bank and Carmen's. Sarah, get back inside. We'll take care of this."

"Not on your life. She's my—"

A scream startled her. She gripped her cell phone. "Emma! Nick, that came from the clearing between the diner and—"

"Got it. Just south of Gerard and me. We're on our way. Get back inside!"

Despite his words, Sarah disconnected and plunged into the darkness. She stumbled over a rock and grabbed a tree for support.

A vicious spate of barking echoed through the trees, and Emma screamed again. Brush and vines scraped Sarah's skin as she ran toward the sound. She broke through the thick trees into an opening where a dim light filtered through the woods onto two figures wrestling in the grass. One of those figures was Emma. In seconds, a furious dog joined the fight.

Sarah ran forward with a cry and shoved the attacker from atop her daughter as Nina snarled and grabbed his arm from the other side.

He grasped Sarah's throat. "Get this beast off me before I shoot her!"

The light revealed the hate-filled scowl of Billy Parker.

Stunned by surprise, Sarah hesitated. "Billy?"

Nina bit at his leg and he shouted an epithet. Sarah jerked away from him, scraped her shoe down the inside of his shin and kicked up with her knee so hard he doubled over.

He backhanded her across the face, knocking her down. Nina attacked him again. Sarah scrambled to Emma's side but could see nothing in the darkness.

"Honey? Emma? Wake up, please!"

Emma didn't move. Nina grunted, then cried out in pain.

In anguish and horror, Sarah kicked up at Billy with all her might and felt her shoe impact bone. With a snarl he pulled out a semiautomatic and aimed it at Emma's head. Sarah lunged for the gun, but a bright light illuminated them and a shout reached her from the edge of the woods.

"Sarah!" It was Nick. "Get down, Sarah!"

She dropped to the soft earth beside Emma, covering her daughter with her own body as a shot rang through her ears. She jerked, but felt no pain. She looked up to find Billy bleeding from his chest. His weapon dropped from his hand onto the muddy ground, and he fell beside it like a bag of sand.

Sarah gagged at the sight and the coppery smell as she pulled Emma into her arms. "Honey? Emma? Oh, baby, please talk to me."

Nina whimpered and crawled over to them as footsteps thudded across the clearing.

"Sarah?" Nick called. "Are you two okay?"

Emma gasped and moaned. Sarah touched her daughter's cheek as terror and love shot through her like hot lead.

"Honey, did he hurt you? Did you hit your head?" She felt tears on Emma's face.

"Sis?"

"I'm right here."

"I hit my head again. Nick said—"

"Nick was scaring you," he said. "I'm sorry." He dropped to his knees beside them.

As he did a head check on their daughter, Sarah felt such a rush of trust and peace. This was right.

The flashing lights of a police cruiser reflected from surrounding trees, and the loud, single call of a siren announced its arrival in Jolly Mill. Another figure came walking toward them across the clearing.

"I just talked to Petra." It was Alec. He sounded breathless and agitated.

"That's Billy." Sarah stood up and pointed toward the fallen man. "He attacked Emma. What on earth is happening here? Why would he—"

"Because she's Nick's daughter." Alec's weary, roughened voice seemed forced from him. "Petra told me more than I wanted to hear. I left Gerard with her. Couldn't take any more. We'll have more police cars here before long."

"Then tell me why Billy Parker would attack my

daughter." Sarah glanced at the silent, cooling body of Nick's cousin.

"Will Parker always pointed to Nick as the kind of man he wanted his son to be," Alec said. "Billy rebelled."

"That's no reason to hurt our daughter." Nick helped Emma sit up.

"Where's Nina?" Emma asked. "Is she hurt?"

The dog whimpered and nudged Emma's hand.

Sarah wanted to go to them, to turn her back on everyone else and be with Nick and Emma, but she needed answers. "Alec, we need to know what she said to you."

"I'm sorry. I should've picked up on some of this sooner." Alec shook his head. "Usually I can read people pretty well, but—"

"That's hard to do when you're falling in love." Sarah felt badly for Alec, but she still needed answers.

"When Petra came to Jolly Mill the first time, Nick, you were kind to her when some of the other kids weren't," he said. "She crushed on you, even though Billy fell head over heels for her."

"He was looking for her the night of the party," Sarah said.

"He heard her asking for Nick. You can imagine that for Billy that had to be a huge kick in the gut."

"He never said anything to me." Nick took off his jacket and wrapped Emma with it.

"He didn't have time to act on it before you left for college, and with you gone, he settled down."

Nick helped Emma to stand, then put an arm around Sarah and drew them both close. "If Petra didn't kill Cindy or Chaz, does that mean Billy did?"

"He told her today that he never stopped loving her, and he'd proved it by covering for her." Alec's voice broke for just a second. "When Chaz questioned Billy about the chafing dishes being too close to the gas lines when he and Petra catered the retreat, Billy went to Petra and started asking questions. He knew how Petra felt about Mark. Sorry, Sarah."

"So he killed anyone who could connect the first explosion back to her," she said. "What about Emma? She was no threat."

Alec's shoulders slumped. He shook his head. "I'm sorry, guys, but when Emma walked into the diner this morning, I could see both of you in her so clearly, I mouthed off something about how she must be your kid. I guess he must have snapped. He had to have overheard me asking Carol where Emma'd gone off to, and so he used the cavern to reach her before we could. Petra was working on her new concoction in the basement near the cavern entrance, and she saw his footprints in the flour and spices."

The crackle of tree limbs and the crush of last year's leaves reached them from the direction of the cruiser, which was parked behind Alec's car. Gerard was walking toward them.

"Deputy's here. Ambulance coming. You all okay?"

"Billy's dead," Nick said.

The reality of it hit Sarah. She burst into tears and buried her face into Nick's shoulder.

Sarah awakened the next morning with a feeling of deep sadness and unbound gratitude as she glanced from her hospital cot to see Emma resting peacefully in the bed. And on the other side of Emma, Nick was stretched out on a sleeping chair, watching their daughter as if nothing in the world had ever been so precious to him.

Once upon a time, Sarah had thought love could conquer all. Until last night.

A nurse knocked on the door, bringing breakfast trays for each of them, but Sarah didn't have much of an appetite this morning.

Nick eased up from the chair with a frown when Sarah pushed her tray aside. "I think Billy and Petra are still harming others," he said softly.

Emma opened sleep-clouded eyes, saw the food and raised her bed. "I'm starved!"

Nick's gaze softened on their daughter, then he looked at Sarah. She couldn't look away, and she also couldn't hide the sadness that gripped her. Their attempts to explain all these years of secrecy to Emma had not worked.

Closing her eyes, Sarah recalled Emma's words

to her last night. "My parents are gone, and no one's ever going to take their place."

"I know that's how you feel now," Sarah had told her. "And we have a lot of things to work out, but you have a father and grandfather you never knew, and since you need them now more than ever, it's best you have the chance to heal here. In Jolly Mill."

Sarah would never forget the expression of sorrow in her daughter's eyes at that moment last night. "You've had your time with me for sixteen years, Sarah. I need some quality time with them." She swallowed. "Without you."

Sarah felt the plunge of a knife into her heart. "You want me to return to Sikeston."

Emma held her gaze as tears dripped down her face. "If you really love me, you'll give me this. For the summer."

Those words had haunted Sarah's dreams all night.

Nick watched fresh lines of grief shadow Sarah's eyes, and he wanted nothing more than to take her into his arms and hold her and never let her go. But Sarah'd promised Emma that she would leave today. He'd been unable to argue her out of it.

How paradoxical that if the explosions hadn't happened, he and Dad might never have known about Emma. He knew he couldn't travel back in time to stop the killing, but he could move forward. Dad had a new reason for living after losing Mom, and so did Nick. The only problem—the horrible problem—was losing Sarah. Yesterday there'd been no time to consider the consequences of Sarah's silence all these years. He'd have expected to experience some outrage at being kept from his daughter, at his Mom's having been robbed of a granddaughter. The only anger he felt toward her was that she was leaving. All the words of reassurance he'd spoken to her—hadn't they affected her at all? Yesterday he'd been ready to marry her and give Emma her own, true parents for the first time in her life, but Sarah wouldn't cooperate.

Emma had held on to him for long moments last night in the hospital room. She'd kissed him and Dad on the check, held on to Dad, told them both she was so glad they were in her life.

And Sarah? She'd stood at the far corner of the private room, the pain in her expression palpable, as it was now.

Emma touched Nick's arm. "Want some of my bacon?"

Though he loved this child of his with a power that overwhelmed him, he wanted to have a long, hard talk with her. She had to see what she was doing to Sarah, but the paradox was that Sarah wouldn't allow him to do so. Until she was gone, he couldn't say the words that would change Emma's mind about Sarah staying.

"Sleep last night?" he asked Emma. He hoped her conscience hadn't allowed it.

She shook her head.

Good. "Me, neither." He gestured to Sarah. "You know it wouldn't be safe to start out on a five-hour drive across the state when you're sleep deprived."

He noticed Emma's hand stop with her fork halfway to her mouth. He wanted her to say something, anything, to prevent this travesty.

"No problem. I slept." Sarah shoved the tray away and stood up, smoothing her shirt and jeans, running her fingers through her hair. Even rumpled and sleepy eyed, she looked wonderful to him, and he knew the way he felt about her right now wasn't going to change.

Sarah had never been one to wallow in guilt, except when it came to Emma. Right now, as she stood facing Nick and Emma, the guilt and agony of loss were tearing her to pieces inside. The only thing that kept these emotions from destroying her was Nick. She could see in his eyes that he didn't want her to go. Those dark eyes gave her hope in the midst of blackness.

"I've signed a form so you or Edward or Carmen can provide or seek healthcare for Emma," she told Nick as she sat down to pull on her shoes.

Nick didn't respond. She looked up to find him watching Emma, whose eyes had overflowed with tears.

"Sweetheart, I don't want to leave you," she told Emma.

"It's just for the summer."

Sarah bit her tongue. She knew the child would not change her mind. But after summer, then what? Would Emma decide she wanted to stay here in Jolly Mill for good?

FIFTEEN

It was late July by the time Sarah Russell edited the final chapter of her third novel in as many years. She sat back in her spine-support chair, stretching her muscles. Instead of reveling in the joy of accomplishment, she stared around her study at the walls of books that hovered over her. All she saw at the moment was emptiness. It had been two months since she'd left her daughter with Nick and Edward.

She could still hear those wonderful men, their voices gentle as they begged her to stay. Carmen had gathered her friends together in an attempt to convince Sarah not to listen to a confused sixteen-year-old girl.

Sarah continued to wonder if she'd done the right thing, even though she'd heard from Nick and Edward often, and Emma emailed her several times a day, and all seemed well.

She recalled driving home with a shredded heart and a spirit of gloom. John, bless him, had followed in a two-car convoy, making her stop every couple of hours for a break and time to talk. Last month, however, when Gerard Vance offered him a job in the newly developed police department—where he would be close to Lynley Marshal—he'd returned to Jolly Mill for good.

Sarah missed him like crazy, but she was happy her cousin had found love again.

She missed Nick as she'd missed him for sixteen years. If Emma weren't thriving with the love of her father and grandfather—and they weren't thriving with her there—she might have wished she'd never returned to Jolly Mill. Might have.

On a whim, she pulled out another manuscript she'd printed recently—it was a compilation of all the emails she and Nick had sent to one another during the past two months. It was thicker than any of her novels. To her surprise, Nick had proven to have a way with words, and she'd discovered she would rather write to him than work on her imaginary stories and beloved characters. At least now she felt there might be a "someday" for her.

The tears had ended about a month after her return home. Though she still missed her parents, and Emma, and wanted badly to be in Jolly Mill with the man she'd never stopped loving, she was gaining perspective again. Hope was a powerful motivator. Nick had given her that.

He and Edward could have happily settled in with

Emma and left Sarah out in the cold, but their posts and lengthy phone calls to her, their emails, their caring hearts, had helped her feel that despite the miles, she was not alone.

Time for lunch, and Sarah was padding barefoot into the kitchen for a salad when the telephone rang. She read the caller ID with surprise. Why on earth was Shelby calling her?

She answered with trepidation. Her sister did, after all, live in Africa, and with all the wild animals and civil wars, it wasn't the safest of places. Telephone calls from Tanzania always frightened Sarah a little.

"Shelby?"

"Hi, sis."

"Everything okay?"

"We're fine here. Well, okay, maybe I'm not fine, but it's my own fault, and you know how stubborn I can be."

Sarah held out the phone, looked at it with a frown, then returned the receiver to her ear. "Huh?"

"Emma's been nagging me for two months to make amends for all these years I've...well...been mad at you. I just called to say I'm sorry, and I know it's long overdue, and it was never your fault that you got pregnant in the first place. Somehow Emma figured out why I've been mad, and that kid doesn't let up."

"Did she tell you what happened in Jolly Mill?"

"She's told me everything. She's your little champion. Let me tell you, sis, your daughter adores you with all her heart."

Really? "That's what people do who love me? Get as far away from me as they can? You to Africa, Emma to Jolly Mill, Mom and Dad to heaven?"

"No, honey. That's not it at all. I didn't leave you because I was angry with you. I left because I was called to serve where I was needed. Anyway, now I'm calling you to say I'm sorry, and that I love you, and that you never did anything to deserve the treatment you received."

Sarah stood staring out the kitchen window at the overgrown garden in the backyard. What on earth had made her think she had a green thumb?

"Sarah?"

"Um, yes, I hear you." All she could think about was Emma being her champion. "Sorry, I'm still catching up."

"I have a lot of growing up to do," Shelby said.

Sarah waited. Her experience with her sister in the past had been apologies transforming into yet more recriminations.

"You know, we used to get along," Shelby said.

"Yes, we did."

"I want that again."

Yeah, but for how long? "That would be nice."

"And it's occurred to me that blaming you for something that wasn't your fault was childish and unacceptable. I am, after all, a missionary. That means I'm supposed to live my life as an example for others. How can I do that when I can't even love and cherish my own twin sister? Is that twisted, or what?"

"Wow, Emma must have really lit into you."

There was a soft sigh. "Sarah, I love you. I admire you, and though I used to be disappointed when I discovered we weren't ever going to be perfect images of one another, someday I want to be like you. I don't know if that'll ever happen, but there's one thing I can do right now to start making up for the way I've treated you."

Sarah's stomach growled. "Okay, I don't need you to grovel. We're fine. I love you, too, and—"

"Would you shut up a minute? I need you to glance in the mirror and make sure you don't have spinach between your teeth."

"I haven't eaten since breakfast. Besides, why would—"

"Eggs, then. Just do it!"

Impatient, Sarah did as she was told. "Now what?"

"Then go to your front door and look outside."

"Why?"

"Do it!"

Sarah smiled. That was the bossy sister she'd always known. Typically, she would rebel, but this time she opened the door. She gasped. There on the porch stood Nick and Emma.

"You didn't check in the mirror, did you?" Shelby asked.

"None of your business."

"Just so you know, this was all Emma's idea."

"It was?"

"Yes. I wish I had her maturity. I'm hanging up now. Love you."

"Love you too, sis."

Sarah set her phone down beside the door, rushed out onto the front porch and fell into the arms of the two people she loved most in all the world. Her family.

Nick kissed her as if he would never let her go. Emma clung to her so tightly Sarah thought she might not be able to catch her breath, but when she came up for air, Nick held out three small jewelry boxes.

"First, let me say that I like the eternity ring best, because it represents us so well," Nick said.

"But I liked the traditional solitaire, two-carat diamond," Emma said.

"We also thought you might like to choose something different, so the other box has a folded catalog of choices," Nick said.

Sarah allowed her heart to pound as she studied the boxes without opening them. "May I ask what, exactly, you two are talking about? Because in all our emails and phone conversations and letters, I don't recall any kind of invitation."

"You mean, as in, will you marry me?" Nick asked. "Because I love you."

"And I love you, sis…Mom." Emma swallowed and her face puckered. Her eyes filled. "I'm sorry I hurt you. I understand everything so much better. Dad and Edward have helped."

Sarah looked at Nick. "Dad and Mom?" She hugged Emma. "Honey, you had a dad and mom. Are you sure that's what you want to call us?"

"I told her that as long as she honored us as her parents, she could call us what she wanted," Nick said. "This was what she chose. And, Sarah, I wish I'd known the moment you conceived so we could have battled all the hardships of young, inexperienced parents working their way through school with the help of four doting grandparents."

"We can't change the past."

"We have a future, though."

"Mom," Emma said softly, "will you marry Dad? I don't think he can live without you."

For the first time in a month, Sarah felt tears in her eyes. Her daughter had called her Mom.

"Well, we can't have a man dying because of me, can we?" she asked as those dratted tears dripped down her face once again. "I guess I'll take the eternity ring because I can't imagine us not being together for eternity."

Nick caught his breath, as if he'd been afraid she wouldn't accept. He wrapped her in his strong arms, and he whispered "I love you" in her ear.

Her life had suddenly filled to overflowing, and she knew it would be that way from now through eternity.

* * * * *

Dear Reader,

We all have skeletons in our closets. Some are mistakes that we made in innocence that had tragic repercussions. Other mistakes are not so innocent—they are sins. God can forgive them as long as we recognize what we've done, that we were out of the Father's will, and turn back to Him. Will we still suffer for those bad choices in this life? My experience has been maybe, but we won't for eternity if we turn to Christ. That's the vital part of sin—turning from it. And God will never stop loving me no matter what.

My friends know me well enough to be braced at any time for me to reveal a deep, shocking secret about my past to anyone I happen to be talking to at the time. I'm not afraid to admit I blew my life to smithereens when I was a teenager and brought shame to myself and my family. My issue wasn't an out-of-wedlock pregnancy, but it was rebellion, running away from home, experimenting with drugs. I lived my own way, and only much later did I suffer the real consequences that came from living my way. I caused others pain, as well, due to my bad choices, as Emma discovered once she's stepped over the line. In *Collateral Damage,* my heroine, Sarah, Emma's secret mother, pays for mistakes that were made in innocence when someone spiked her and the hero's soda with ecstasy. She lives with the consequences of that night, despite her innocence, and she allows God to turn what could have been a painful price into something beautiful. Did her parents handle the situation properly? How can we judge? They did the best they could in a horrible situation—they brought new life into the world and nurtured it. Isn't that the way we should live our lives? God wants our honesty. We don't cover up our ugliness, we give it to God, just as it is, as we are, and ask Him to fix it. He will. He does with me. Think of how often He'll do that with you.

Open your heart to God and give Him all the truth about yourself, good and bad. You'll be surprised how He comforts and guides.

Much love from

Hannah Alexander

Questions for Discussion

1. Have you ever run away from home? If so, please tell us about it, good and bad.

2. Have you done something that shocked the community? What did your friends and neighbors say? Were there rumors? How did you feel about those rumors? Do you feel the rumors might be as bad a sin as the rebellion shown in running away, or in an unwed pregnancy?

3. Everyone who knows about Sarah's pregnancy has forgiven her long since Emma was born, except for her twin sister. Why do you think Shelby, a dedicated missionary, would hold a grudge for so long?

4. In *Collateral Damage,* young Emma does not know she still has a mother and father who will never leave her this side of death, and yet she's grieving the death of the only parents she's ever known—her grandparents. How could Sarah have helped her through this?

5. Could the whole situation have been handled differently from the beginning?

6. When you hear the term *collateral damage* in

view of a murder, what does that tell you about the killer?

7. Are there degrees of sin?

8. Should Sarah have told Nick about her suspicions about Emma being his child? Please explain your answer.

9. Nick is struggling with his disappointment not only at being slapped with a frivolous lawsuit, but about an unfaithful wife. Do you sometimes think life should be more fair? What do you think he would be like if he hadn't endured those disappointments?

10. How did you feel about so many of the citizens of Jolly Mill carrying weapons? Do they seem trustworthy?

11. What would you do if you lived in an unpoliced community? How would you protect yourself and your loved ones?

12. How did you feel about Emma asking Sarah to return to Sikeston without her? Did Sarah overreact?

13. Was Sarah overprotective? Should she have been allowed to raise her daughter as her own?

14. Was Sarah's angry sister fit to be a missionary when she held such bitterness in her heart about Sarah?

15. Do you have siblings who judge you harshly? Is there something you can do to heal that breach, or do you feel that you can lovingly release them to God's care and back out of their lives as much as possible?

LARGER-PRINT BOOKS!

GET 2 FREE
LARGER-PRINT NOVELS
PLUS 2 FREE
MYSTERY GIFTS

Love Inspired

Larger-print novels are now available...

YES! Please send me 2 FREE LARGER-PRINT Love Inspired® novels and my 2 FREE mystery gifts (gifts are worth about $10). After receiving them, if I don't wish to receive any more books, I can return the shipping statement marked "cancel." If I don't cancel, I will receive 6 brand-new novels every month and be billed just $5.24 per book in the U.S. or $5.74 per book in Canada. That's a savings of at least 23% off the cover price. It's quite a bargain! Shipping and handling is just 50¢ per book in the U.S. and 75¢ per book in Canada.* I understand that accepting the 2 free books and gifts places me under no obligation to buy anything. I can always return a shipment and cancel at any time. Even if I never buy another book, the two free books and gifts are mine to keep forever.

122/322 IDN F49Y

Name	(PLEASE PRINT)

Address	Apt. #

City	State/Prov.	Zip/Postal Code

Signature (if under 18, a parent or guardian must sign)

Mail to the Harlequin® Reader Service:
IN U.S.A.: P.O. Box 1867, Buffalo, NY 14240-1867
IN CANADA: P.O. Box 609, Fort Erie, Ontario L2A 5X3

**Are you a current subscriber to Love Inspired books
and want to receive the larger-print edition?
Call 1-800-873-8635 or visit www.ReaderService.com.**

* Terms and prices subject to change without notice. Prices do not include applicable taxes. Sales tax applicable in N.Y. Canadian residents will be charged applicable taxes. Offer not valid in Quebec. This offer is limited to one order per household. Not valid for current subscribers to Love Inspired Larger-Print books. All orders subject to credit approval. Credit or debit balances in a customer's account(s) may be offset by any other outstanding balance owed by or to the customer. Please allow 4 to 6 weeks for delivery. Offer available while quantities last.

Your Privacy—The Harlequin® Reader Service is committed to protecting your privacy. Our Privacy Policy is available online at www.ReaderService.com or upon request from the Harlequin Reader Service.

We make a portion of our mailing list available to reputable third parties that offer products we believe may interest you. If you prefer that we not exchange your name with third parties, or if you wish to clarify or modify your communication preferences, please visit us at www.ReaderService.com/consumerchoice or write to us at Harlequin Reader Service Preference Service, P.O. Box 9062, Buffalo, NY 14269. Include your complete name and address.

LILPDIR13R

ReaderService.com

Manage your account online!

- Review your order history
- Manage your payments
- Update your address

---

*We've designed
the Harlequin® Reader Service
website just for you.*

Enjoy all the features!

- Reader excerpts from any series
- Respond to mailings and
  special monthly offers
- Discover new series available to you
- Browse the Bonus Bucks catalog
- Share your feedback

Visit us at:
ReaderService.com